D1599842

In Sickness and in Hell
-a collection of unusual stories-

Stefan Barkow

FoxBo Books
Chesterton, Indiana

ISBN: 0692288333
ISBN-13: 978-0692288337

To those who encouraged me to explore, and to those willing to look at what I brought back. Thank you all.

CONTENTS

ACKNOWLEDGMENTS

Even a short collection requires significant effort by more than just the author. Thanks go to the members of the Blank Slate writing group for their feedback on a number of these stories over the years and to Taylor Ricks for her concept art. I'd also like to thank Peter Appel, Denise Barkow, Ben Gillman, and Drew Tallackson for their edits and suggestions as this collection took form. Kate Murray and Hallie Orgel I thank for their help respectively behind and before the camera in the making of the cover photo. Finally, I'd like to thank my wife Melissa for her constant encouragement and faith in me.

MYSTRAL

When I wake, the drums have already begun. I sit up in my nest of furs to listen. There is a rustling from just outside my family's tent, along the southern-facing side.

"Tuluk?" I say.

The sound stops. "I am here, Sister," says my older brother, Tuluk. His voice sounds strained, as though he regrets waking me. He must have hoped that I would sleep through the ritual.

I hear the sand beneath his feet as he comes around the tent, and then the flap of the animal skin that hangs over the doorway when he pushes it aside.

From where I sit, I hold out my hands to him. He comes to me and takes both of my hands in one of his, pulling me up.

"You came for your drum?" I say.

"Yes."

"Let me touch it?"

He hesitates. I know that he doesn't want me to, for fear the gods will be offended, but he presses it into my hands anyway.

I had forgotten how heavy it was. It is as big as the basket that holds my clothes, with tall sides and a round top three times the size of my hand. I rub the smooth deerskin, then the

1

rough leather thongs woven over the thick wood of the drum's body to keep the skin taut. I tuck the drum under my right arm and lift my hand, but Tuluk sees what I am about to do and catches my wrist. He pulls the drum from my arms, and I do not resist him.

"Is father at the idol with the others?" I ask.

"Yes," he answers. He is farther away from me now. Near the entrance.

"And mother?"

"I don't have time, Mystral. I must go." Another hesitation. Then, quieter, "They're starting soon."

"Please," I say, "help me dress."

But instead I hear a soft *thunk* when his drum strikes one of the thin tree trunks that give our tent shape, and the sound of the animal skin falling closed behind him, muffling the drumming from outside once more.

Alone again, I sit. Beside my furs I feel for the familiar texture of my basket. Carefully, I take each bit of clothing out one by one until I find what I want. Buried at the bottom, wrinkled but clean, the only dress I have ever owned.

I slip it over my head. The fabric is soft. It has no sleeves, and when I stand the hem grazes my knees. It was a gift from my mother. She tells me it is a vibrant green, like the broad-bladed grasses that grow to the north of our village. These words mean nothing to me, but I have never told her that.

Outside, I crouch low so that I won't trip over anything. To my left there is the crackling of a fire. To my right, more drums have joined those of the elders. With one voice, the drums call to the gods, hoping to get their attention. Our sacrifice must not go unnoticed or else we will all die.

I release the waxy skin of my family's tent and head toward the idol. Where the drummers are. Where the elders are. Where the sacrifice will be.

I shuffle forward with my hands in front of me, letting the coarse sand sift between my toes. The air is cold on my bare arms. Now that I'm away from my tent, I can hear the rustling of a dying field of wheat to my left. It is a thousand death rattles, the last painful moment of life that goes on forever as the dry wind tortures the stalks. Like my people, dying the slow death.

Our village is small. In just a few minutes I'm nearly to the stone idol of Yllin, god of rain. With their drums my people are calling with one voice to the gods to look to us, and they are offering our best as a sacrifice. They are not calling for me.

Yllin stands in our village as a pale white rock. In this form, he is taller than I am. I do not know how tall he is; I cannot reach above him, so to me it is as though he goes on forever into the sky. Perhaps he is the sky, and that is how he brings his waters. I do not know. Even under the hot sun, Yllin is cool and moist to the touch. In the moonlight, I am told that Yllin sparkles.

For three weeks, I have gone to Yllin and pressed my hand against his firm body. For three weeks, he has not been cool or damp. Now, they say the streams flow only with dust and sand. We have gone without water in offering to him, but he has not returned to us or answered our pleas. Tonight, the elders have said that we must make the ritual of offering.

It is meant to be a secret who the elders will choose, but I know the one that they have picked. Her name is Aethna, and she is the most beautiful girl I have ever touched. We are not meant to talk of such things, but Aethna tells me thoughts that she does not tell the others. I think she forgets that I can speak. To her I am an invalid, capable of nothing. She is my best friend.

I know when I have come to the fire's edge because even over the pounding of the drums there is a murmur of disapproval from those nearest me. I heard my mother talk of this when my father was not around to prevent her. She said that some of the elders spoke of offering me to Yllin instead. I know I had heard pride in her voice when she said it, but that pride was so quick to fade I must remind myself even now that I did not imagine it. They would be free of my burden, the elders had argued. My mother heard only that they thought her

3

daughter enough to satiate the god. But others said I was unfit for the task, that offering one such as me would offend Yllin. Those voices convinced the others, and now I hear them all around me, whispering.

A thin hand finds my arm, pulls me away from the warmth of the fires. It is my mother, sent hurriedly by my father to stop me from disturbing the ceremony. Though I did not see Yllin, I know he was there before me, somewhere, his stone skin dry in the fire's light, but I am led into the shadow of the meeting hall so that I will not be in the way. I wonder if the moon is out right now. I wonder if Yllin is sparkling in the light he borrows from his brother.

The ground shivers beneath my feet. The drums beat louder. My mother's warm breath is in my ear. "Stay, Mystral. Stay," she says. She gives me commands as if I am one of the dogs, and I obey her. She leaves my side and goes to sit with the rest of my family.

Alone again, I crouch. I grip the smooth stones that are the foundation of the meeting hall, letting my fingers map their texture as I listen to the drummers. I pretend for a time that I can make out the sound of each man's hands on the skins. I hear the powerful strokes of Iedneth the elder, and I hear Tuluk's careful work. I hear my father's violent blows as well, and I know without question that it is him because he has beaten me with equal passion.

In the sand and dirt and stone beneath my feet I can tell how badly the land hurts, how thirsty it is to drink of Aethna's sacrifice. It seems forever before they bring her out.

I do not know where she is, but I know that she is unclothed and beautiful. The elders have spent the day preparing her, starting with the last of our water and then with the oils that will make her skin glow in the moonlight as if she were made of the same pure stone as Yllin himself. I wish that I could touch her, because I know that Aethna is afraid.

And I wish that I could take her place.

I hear the drums shift as a passageway is made through the gathered men. Aethna, naked and pure, walks in bare feet towards Yllin. Aethna, naked and pure, kneels. Her fine straight hair parts across her neck as she bows her head into her folded hands.

The drums call louder; the sacrifice is ready, they say, our best is before you, look on us and give pity, Yllin! Take from us and give back, as you promised you would to the fathers of our ancestors!

It is all a lie, but only I know this. Aethna and I. She told me, during a time when she had forgotten that I too had words, how afraid she was. She did not want to be offered to Yllin, she said. She did not believe in him.

The drums beat faster, my people's need given form by the desperate rhythm. One man rises from the circle and crosses the smooth sand to stand beside Aethna. There is a knife in his right hand. I hear the clouds pause in their journey across the sky, transfixed by what is about to happen.

What if I spoke now? They put me in the shadows and pretend that they can't see me, but they have called the gods, and the gods are listening. What if I were to scream out Aethna's blasphemies? They could not sacrifice her then; it would surely offend Yllin. They would need another. Maybe they would pick me, and I would have my chance to serve Yllin, to be the savior my people seek. If it be your will, I pray to Yllin, give me the courage to speak!

But even with my mouth open I cannot bring forth the words. Instead, I listen. With all of my being, I listen. But Aethna is not crying.

My empathy becomes anger. Aethna lied. She told me she was afraid. She told me that I should be the one offered to Yllin. She knew how pure my faith and how great my desire. What was my sin? She had echoed my own thoughts when she said it, quietly and out away from the village where no one else could hear. "You have such beautiful eyes, Mystral," she said, "pale and pure and white, as if you are always looking to Yllin."

But Aethna was chosen instead of me. For her beauty, and for her value to our village. She will be missed. I am not worthy. I am not beautiful. I am a burden, able to give nothing to the village, not even my life. Not even my love.

I imagine the heavy blade swinging swiftly down through the dry air, the man behind it obscured by an intricate mask I have never been allowed to explore with my hands. He will not miss, unless Aethna moves. But I know Aethna now; her lie has revealed her truth, and I know that she is happy to take my place, to perform the sacred duty that would have been my only contribution to my family and to my village.

The drums are silent now.

It is a quiet sound a soul makes when it's freed from the body, and I wonder if anyone hears it but me. It is a peaceful sound a soul makes, not so much like a last breath going out as like a first breath coming in. It is the sound I hear Aethna's soul make as it rises to plead with our god.

The drums begin again, but now they are not the drums of my people. They are the drums of Yllin, his strong fingers striking the dry, stretched surface of our world a hundred times a thousand around me. The sound of my people's joy is in the air as they dance with the rains. The ground beneath my feet drinks with greed, just as it drank of Aethna's blood moments ago.

I know now without question that the god of rain is listening. And I know now, without question, that to him I am nothing.

Alone, I stand as Aethna's rain strikes me in the face. I pretend the drops are my own tears, but I know better; my eyes cannot make water, just as my soul cannot bring rain. I slip my dress off of my shoulders. It falls around my feet and I leave it where it falls, wrinkled but clean. Naked, I walk north out of the village. I do not know if anyone sees me leave, but if they do they do not try to stop me.

Aethna will live forever as the girl who died. But the blind girl? I will die alone, having never lived at all.

THESE WOODS ARE DARK

Timmy stood alone on the old wooden porch. A flicker of motion—the slightest sense of a leaf moving in the darkness or of a vine swaying in a stray breeze—brought young Timmy's eye from the warm light of the cabin to the deep dark of the woods around him. Unbidden, a forgotten nursery rhyme came into his head:

> *These woods are dark,*
> *These woods are deep;*

Timmy crossed his arms, shuffled his feet, and leaned against a support timber. It was a rhyme he had read a few years ago. He couldn't remember all of it.

> *These woods are dark,*
> *These woods are deep;*

He had never heard it spoken out loud. He had never given it the weight of speech. Still, the words felt as ominous as the pitch-press of night that only moments before had seemed like a welcome release from the noise of his family.

Timmy stepped off of the porch, lost in thought as he tried to summon the rest of the rhyme from memory. The words refused to come. Timmy tried it out loud:

"These woods are dark," he recited. "These woods are deep—"

But again, memory failed him. Frustrated, Timmy threw a branch into the woods. He heard it land somewhere among the fallen leaves. He looked back over his shoulder at the cabin. He saw the sharp profiles of his parents projected as shadows onto the curtains that covered the cabin's windows. In the next window over he could make out the shapes of his older brother and sister, who were further away from the fireplace, playing a game together.

Timmy turned back to the woods and a branch hit him in the face. Caught off guard, he fell backwards onto the dead leaves that carpeted the muddy ground. He felt tears in his eyes from the sting of the pine needles. Rubbing away the pain with a small, dirty fist, he got to his feet again and kicked the tree.

"These woods are dark," Timmy repeated. "These woods are deep—"

But for a third time he couldn't find the rest of the words.

Timmy tried picturing the yellowed piece of paper—no, it hadn't been paper, it had been something thicker, with texture. Though the words themselves still wouldn't come, the details came back quickly as he rebuilt the vacation in his mind: He had found the book on his first visit here with his parents. He had been six at the time. There had been a lock holding the book shut, but he had used his father's pocketknife to jimmy it open.

Timmy pushed a low-hanging branch out of his face.

These woods are filled,
The quiet ones say...

Those weren't the next lines in the rhyme, but Timmy was sure they came somewhere later. The print had been hard to read, written in curling letters of blue and red and gold, but

Timmy recalled with pride that his six year old self had refused to ask anyone else for help. He closed his eyes shut hard and tried to remember with all of his might what the words on that single page had said:

"These woods are dark," Timmy whispered. "These woods are deep—" Again, he paused. He strained his mind to uncurl the lines of the letters. Then, "—These woods grow closer when you sleep," he said at last. His body shivered.

As those words left his lips, the next set came into his mind, as clear as if the book itself were spread before him.

> "These woods are filled,
> The quiet ones say,
> With a spirit dark;
> An ancient Fae."

Again, the next set of lines sprang into Timmy's mind as soon as the last had left his mouth and Timmy, remembering too late the warning they bore, clamped both hands over his mouth in terror.

The rhyme came back to him in full now. He had read it over and over and over and then forced the lock back into place and hidden the book in the dirt beneath the floorboard where he had found it. He hadn't told anyone else in his family about the rhyme. Fear had kept him silent, and by the next morning it had all seemed like a bad dream. Until tonight, when the memories came rushing back.

Timmy turned in a small circle, his hands still pressed to his open mouth, his eyes wide with apprehension.

At first, there was only the wind in the branches and the whisper of the leaves around him. But as he listened, he heard the voices of countless children in that whisper, and felt her arms reaching for him from within those branches.

"And if you speak these words so dear—" Timmy thought he heard the forest chanting around him, *"Then, little child, these woods will hear."*

Timmy turned towards the cabin and ran as hard as his legs could carry him. It seemed much further from him now than when he walked outside to get away from his family. Around him, the forest went on with its litany:

*"And come she will
To take you in,
And never more
Go home again."*

Timmy tripped on a root, flew through the air, and collided with the bottom stair of the old wooden porch. The door opened and his mother looked out through a crack of light. "Timmy!" she said, "Where have you been?" But Timmy was still listening to the voices of the lost children:

*"So, little one,
Forget what we say.
Else you shall meet
Viktoria the Fae..."*

"Timothy, I was worried," his mother said as she picked him up and brushed him off. "Why are you out of breath?"

Nearly too scared to move, Sam forced his head to turn back towards the forest. It looked just as it had when he had stepped off of the porch. Not a single leaf seemed out of place.

"It's time for bed now," his mother said. "Everyone else has already gone to sleep. Go on then, get inside." With a last wary look at the woods, Timmy went inside. His mother shut and locked the door behind him. The click of the deadbolt broke Timmy from his stupor.

"Mom! We have to go home now! I..."

"Shhh!" she whispered, a finger held across her lips. "I told you, everyone else is asleep already! Please, quietly go to your room!"

Timmy made a dash for the floor plank that hid the book, but his mother's hand had him by the collar. "Oh no you

11

don't!" she said. "I don't know what's gotten into you, but it's clear you scared yourself silly playing out there in the dark." She marched him to the room he shared with his brother and sister.

"But—" Timmy began. She silenced him with a slap across the cheek. "I'll not have you talking back to me either, young man! You know better!"

It was no use. Timmy dutifully changed into his pajamas and got into bed. His mother came in to tuck him in.

"Oh Timmy," she said. She was looking down at him much more kindly now that he was in bed and being quiet. "You've let your imagination take you away again, haven't you? But here, look"—she crossed the room and drew the curtain back from the window—"Nothing out there, just a quiet, peaceful evening."

She let the curtain fall back into place and kissed him on the forehead. "Now go to sleep, Timmy."

"Mom…" Timmy said as she was closing the door behind her.

"Not another word, Timmy!" she hissed back. She let out an exasperated sigh. "Everything will be okay in the morning, I promise. Now, go to sleep!"

And she shut the door firmly behind her.

* * *

Half an hour later, Timmy was staring at the curtained window across the room. He thought he had heard something tapping on the glass. He tried to tell himself that it was just the wind, but there weren't any trees close enough to the cabin for a branch to reach. At least, there hadn't been when his mom made him get in bed. Straining his ears, he waited for it to come again, but everything was silent. Then, *tap tap tap*.

Timmy counted his brother's snores until he reached twenty-five. Slipping out from beneath the covers as quietly as he could, Timmy crawled across the rough boards to the window and carefully pulled himself up beside the bottom sill.

Without any light behind them, the thin cotton of the curtains was enough to block any sight of the forest surrounding the cabin.

As slowly and carefully as he could, Timmy pushed aside a tiny corner of the curtain and held one eye up to the opening.

Nothing. Nothing but the trees and the dead leaves and the breeze that made the leaves whisper. Timmy breathed a sigh of relief. But then, he heard the voices of the woods over the sound of his brother's snoring as they recited the final verse:

> *"Her woods are dark,*
> *Her woods are deep;*
> *Her woods grow closer*
> *When you sleep."*

Then the yellow eye of Viktoria the Fae was staring back at Timmy through the corner of the window.

"I've been waiting for you, Timothy," she whispered to him in the silence. "Sleep well, little child. Sleep well…"

WHAT IS LUCY FOR?

Lucy opened her eyes and stood up in the cold room. Across from her, the dim red light of her alarm clock glowed in the darkness. Six a.m. She'd fallen asleep on the floor of her dorm room again, face down between carbon structure diagrams and unbalanced chemical equations.

Walking towards the single, blind-covered window at the end of the room, Lucy rubbed her eyes. Her mind recalled the events of the day before and just as quickly dismissed them; lately, every day seemed better forgotten than remembered. Lucy threw open the blinds, suddenly scared by the darkness all around her.

She gathered her books from the floor, throwing them into a pile and dropping them on the desk on her side of the room.

Lucy's roommate Jackie shifted in the top bunk.

"Damn it, Lucy, why are you so loud? Be a little considerate, will you? I don't have class until ten!"

"Sorry," Lucy mumbled. She and Jackie didn't get along that great. No matter how hard she tried, Lucy always seemed to do something that bothered her university-appointed roommate. It was weird, because at home she had never felt

15

like she was that difficult to live with. Maybe she and Jackie just weren't a good match.

She crossed back across the room and flicked on the small fluorescent light above her mirror. *Never a good match,* she thought into to her reflection as she combed her straight black hair. *Doesn't matter what it is, but it never feels right. And always so—* she pulled a battered hoodie over her head, looking into her own harsh eyes as she pulled up the hood, the cloth causing black shadows to fall across her face—*distant.*

Her life had been changing, but not as she had wanted it to. At long last, here she was at college, away from her family and her home. Surrounded instead by endless cornfields and bunker-like brick buildings. In high school she had never stood out, academically or socially, yet she had never quite fallen through the cracks either. Despite her best efforts she could never force her way beyond what appeared to be her station in life. She had family of course, and people she talked to and people who trusted her, but no one she really called friend. It wore on her constantly, as carrying such a burden would wear on anyone who bore it alone.

She had thought that it would be different at college.

As she stepped down the granite stairs into the low mist and night-formed dew, she hiked her backpack up and tucked her hands into the front pouch of her sweatshirt, the image momentarily reminiscent of a robed monk called to vespers until a break of sun cut through the trees overhead, reminding her that another long day was only just beginning. The light dissipated in the swirling fog at her feet.

There was one thing that Lucy knew for certain though: there was something different about her. She never could find exactly what the cause was, but somehow she always found herself alone in the end. It was never a sudden exodus by those around her, it was not a defined departure. Friends just drifted away. Whenever this happened Lucy would be consumed with self-doubt. *Is it me? Something I did? The way I said something?* But she was alone with no one to answer her questions, and there was nothing for her to do but bear the burden and continue on her path.

She had so *hoped* that it would be different at college.

She had made sure to pick a school far away from home, where no one knew her, where she could start over. It didn't matter. Her curse had followed her, and those that she tried to draw close to always seemed to be pushed further away instead. Thinking on it now, she realized that more than once a friend had seemed much happier once Lucy was out of the picture. It was a thought that drew Lucy closer to the dark ideas of the night before; to the dark thoughts of every night over the last month of her miserable life.

The beauty of fall is sister to the bitter cold, and more often than not the siblings travel hand-in-hand. Lucy's thin hoodie, faded with years of use, couldn't hold back the chill any better than it could levee the bitter emotions flooding her conscience on this silent morning. Bit by bit, the layered protection she'd built up over years of loneliness broke, and her tears fell to mingle with the morning dew. Flinging her backpack away from her, she slumped heavily to the ground. Wracking sobs shuddered through her as she clutched at the earth, the cold grass slipping through her fingers. Her soul cried out with a hundred questions, and each of those questions was the same: *Why?* Why was she alone. Why was she forbidden from happiness. Why was she alive at all.

This at last was all she could take. All her life she had tried, but now she knew she could withstand the crushing despair no longer. There were a hundred ways to escape from this life, and each of them was the same. The cool mist spun in eddies around her body, playing with the shadows of dark thoughts in her mind.

"Are you alright, miss?" a warm voice asked from nearby. Lucy looked up as she brushed loose hair from her eyes. A scholarly looking man sat just ten or so feet from her on a park bench, enjoying the morning air. He had kind eyes which were turned away from the rising sun and compassionately towards her prone form.

Embarrassed, Lucy stood up as she tried to wipe away her tears. "Yes, I'm okay, it's just a difficult week for me."

"My dear, it's only Monday morning. How can a week so freshly started already be categorized so poorly?"

"It's…it's more than just the week, I guess."

The stranger smiled. "Good. To admit is to stand before the gateway of acceptance and—for some—acceptance itself is the gateway to forgiveness. It is the former that applies here, and that is why I've come to see you, Lucy Evans."

Suspicion filled her with foreboding. Not fear, but wariness. "What do you mean you've come to see me? Do I know you?"

"No, but don't be afraid, I won't detain you long. Come, sit by me and take in the glorious light of the rising sun."

Lucy stepped towards him. The mist seemed to grow thicker with each step until she felt as if her feet should find resistance to her movement. She sat at the far end of the isolated bench beneath a large tree, its leafy defenses falling as winter marched ever closer.

"Do you go to school here?" Lucy asked the stranger timidly. Chuckling, he shook his head no. "Do you know me from somewhere else then?" Lucy asked. The stranger watched her out of the corner of his eye, evaluating.

"Not exactly, but I've been monitoring you for some time now. I know a lot about you, but this is the first time we've been allowed to meet in person."

Lucy's anxiety grew as the man went on. She couldn't tell what he was trying to say, and she could no longer see anything beyond the thick fog that had surreptitiously surrounded their sheltered garden.

"You're starting to scare me," she interrupted. "Either tell me what's going on or…or…" Now Lucy heard the first notes of fear enter her voice. She had no clue what she could even threaten him with. Why had she sat down, anyway? She couldn't remember doubting that it was what she should do, she had just followed what he had suggested, like he had power over her somehow.

"Peace, child," the man said as he placed his hand on her arm, "for the Lord is with you."

Through his touch, a long history of lives flashed through her mind like a torrent of water, each life a droplet flowing by too fast to be named, but as a whole she witnessed an unending existence filled with near-despair. And yet through it all Lucy felt herself enveloped in a deep feeling of contentment such as she had never before experienced in her entire life.

A few minutes passed in silence as Lucy's mind caught up with the world. When she had recovered enough to speak again, Lucy looked in wonder at the stranger and asked, "What are you?"

"An angel, of sorts," the man answered. "It's not a very accurate answer, I'm afraid, but it's the easiest and most useful one I can offer you."

"What is going on, what is happening to me?" Lucy asked, more to herself than to him. She felt that she should be more upset, more afraid, but his hand was still on her arm and the feeling of peace still radiated from his touch.

"You asked a question, and it's my job to answer it for you, that is all. You lead an unusual life, child, and you are deserved some explanation as to why.

"Ready then?" the man continued, "Alright, here goes: First of all, I am indeed a servant for the Lord, and I've come to you to steer you away from...well, from a darker path. God has a purpose for all of his children, even the inhuman ones." He paused, and it took her a second to realize that he was referring to her.

"I'm...not human?"

"Not completely. There's no earthly term for what you are, but if you like you can think of yourself as part angel. Mostly, if truth be told. Now then, quick change of topic but it must be done. Do you know of Lucifer?"

"The devil? Of course I do. I went to Sunday school as a child. He's the bad guy, the tempter, the torturer of souls and all that."

The stranger shrugged his broad shoulders in response. "Not quite that cut-and-dry I'm afraid, little one. Think of the question this way: not who, but *what* is Lucifer? What purpose does he serve in the celestial scheme of things?" He watched as her mind worked.

"Well, he's on the other side," she began, slowly. "He represents evil."

"Almost right. Allow me to fill in the holes; I'm sure you will see how obvious they are once pointed out. God sent Jesus, the teacher, to show humans the right way to live their lives, correct? But we know that not everyone learns the same way, and that different ways of teaching are required to reach different types of people. Jesus was the right path, an example of how decisions should be made and how lives should be lived. So what would that make Lucifer?"

"The wrong path?"

"Now you're getting it. You were correct when you said that Lucifer is on the 'other side.' Try thinking of a soul as an object that must be moved. To move it, you either pull it towards you from one side or you—"

"Push it away from the other."

"Precisely. Jesus is an attractive force; Lucifer, a repulsive one, but both serve the purpose of guiding the world towards its proper destination."

"Wait a sec," Lucy interrupted. "Then Lucifer's not really a bad guy, is he? He's being villainized when he's actually helping people. That hardly seems fair to me."

"Not exactly. Don't doubt that Lucifer is evil, but his evil is to fulfill a purpose, the knowledge of which makes it easier for him to bear his own existence. I'll agree that it's unfair though, for he had little choice in the matter. Which brings us to the real point of this visitation." He turned his body fully and faced her directly. His eyes shone with a piercing light as he looked at her.

"What is Lucy for?"

Her mind reeled at the implications of his question. "You weren't quite telling the truth earlier," Lucy said quietly. "I'm no angel. I push people away from the darkness, don't I? I'm repulsive, like Lucifer."

The angel's voice took on a new urgency. "Yes," he said, "you are. But you're forgetting that Lucifer is an angel too, just like you. You're not evil the way he has become though, nor as loathsome. For you in particular it's subtle sins, the smallest of trespasses which bleed the world of goodness one tiny evil at a time: lies, ingratitudes, jealousies and the like. There are thousands of your type all over the world. Without even knowing it, you take on and exemplify the evils and the faults of the people around you—you weren't a bad roommate until you moved in with Jackie, remember?—and seeing it in you steers them away and back to the path they were meant to follow."

The truth behind his words cut her deeply, all of her shadows drawn out and exposed. Once again, Lucy felt tears on her face.

"But it repels them from me. That's why they drift away. That's why they're happier when I'm gone," she said.

"It does," the man admitted. "But they are better for having known you, Lucy, and that is a fact you must hold in your heart and never allow yourself to forget."

He reached out and lifted her chin, forcing her to look him in the eye. Her hood fell back around her shoulders.

"Please understand, dear one, that there is nothing wrong with you, it's just the way you were made. It's what you are meant for." He smiled as he looked at her, but behind his eyes Lucy saw a thought that the angel seemed not to want to say aloud. He released her chin. His voice went quiet again, like that of a patient father speaking to his child.

"Alright, dear one, I'm sorry but the next part is the hardest. Now that you know the truth of your existence, I must offer you with a choice. I cannot sugar coat this contract. Are you ready?"

Lucy nodded her head. The mist swirled violently on the ground around them, but the sparse leaves of the trees remained motionless. There was no sound now but that of her breathing.

He stood and approached her where she sat, gripping her shoulders in his hands. His entrancingly bright eyes were mere inches from her face. She held herself as still as possible, holding his gaze and wondering why even beneath the glow of contentment she was beginning to feel fear.

Then all of a sudden his voice was in her head, loud and echoing, each word reverberating within her.

You were created to guide His people to the correct path. You had no choice, for it is your purpose and it is all that you exist for. You cannot lead a normal human life for you are not one of them.

Her hands were clamped desperately over her ears and her mouth was open. Her body was screaming. The angel went on, relentless.

You must carry this burden alone, armed only with the knowledge that there are others like you, and that your suffering means salvation for His children. There is no life for you but duty. There is no punishment if you reject this, only oblivion. Those are your options. This is your choice. Decide, and your decision shall be done.

And then it was over, his voice was out of her head and Lucy found herself being held, her head tucked into his shoulder and his hand stroking her hair.

After a while, Lucy pulled herself upright on the empty park bench. The stranger was gone. On trembling legs she retrieved her backpack from the ground nearby and walked towards campus. The air was still cold but the sunlight and the shadows had reached a compromise in the mid-morning. Lucy left her hood down, letting her skin absorb the bright world around her. But her mind was still focused inward, contemplating the shadow she had once thought to be a soul.

Six months passed.

Without trying, Lucy continued exemplifying the sins of those around her. Just like normal people, she never realized it was happening until it was too late; everything from anger issues and compulsive lying to addiction, jealousy, and ungratefulness, just as the angel had said.

Following multiple arrests, former classmates and local people from town wrote Lucy off as just another screw-up. She had dropped out of college when she found out she was pregnant five months ago, but she could still be seen around the campus town doing odd jobs and scraping out a living.

She didn't play up her struggles just because she knew the truth of their purpose; that wasn't how it worked. She would've stayed in college, but that wasn't how it worked either. What was needed of her just seemed to come about on its own and Lucy lived on as best she could.

When she wondered how something like her could possibly mother a child, her answer had come in the form of a painful miscarriage.

I should have known, she had thought as the doctors removed her daughter's corpse from her womb. *Mary's son changed the world through his life, so mine was destined to change it through her death.* Lucy had tried to catch a glimpse of her baby, but the nurse had rushed out of the room with the lifeless bundle and Lucy was too weak to call her back. *But how is this a better world now? How could this possibly be His plan?*

Again, oblivion had beckoned as she learned the agony of loss and felt the aching emptiness inside her that she could not escape from. Day after day the pain was with her, dominating all other thoughts and miseries. That was a month ago, now.

But Lucy knew there was something different about her.

She began to suspect the angel had known all along what was coming, that this was the reason he had visited her in the park that day, and not because of anything that had happened to her before. In time, Lucy regained her faith, though she was still haunted by an ache that had yet to begin to fade, if it ever would.

Her only solace was in her thoughts, but at times even these betrayed her. Times like tonight, when the ghost of the daughter she could have had holds hands with the human life

Lucy might have lived and these ghosts refuse to rest, dragging themselves through her head over and over again instead.

She had so hoped that her life would be different.

Tonight Lucy sits in her one-room apartment, crying. Her darkness surrounds her and reminds her that she isn't one of them. But unlike before, now that darkness comforts her, and reminds her of what she is and why she is here. It reminds her that every suffering she endures is for a purpose, that every struggle she is subjected to prevents another from having to endure such pain.

She thinks of the angel and of his gifts to her, he who was created for the sole purpose of protecting her and the others like her. She thinks of her choice, and of her own purpose, and she says her prayers to the setting sun.

* * *

In the morning, a dim light glows in her darkness. Lucy pulls a battered hoodie over her shoulders, raising the hood over her head.

Walking down the stairs from her apartment to the street, she sees some students heading towards campus. As she blends into the group, Lucy eyes the young men and women around her, and starts to guess at their sins.

I LOVED YOU ONCE AND FOREVER
-a binary tale of love and identity-

I LOVED YOU ONCE

"I think I want to take salsa lessons," you told me. You said it so seriously I nearly laughed. But like every time before, it was at that moment when I realized you were no longer the woman I loved.

Even after all these iterations, I still don't understand what happened. But people change as time passes, and I know now that each second carries with it the chance that your best friend will become a complete stranger. I used to love you, I know I did, but that was yesterday when you were still her.

I wonder if you ever think like I do. I wonder if you've ever looked over and wished for a different me back, just as I'm looking at you right now. Seeing you on the couch here, with my arm around you and your head in my lap and the steam rising off our mugs on the living room table, I suspect you've never had such thoughts. I can see in your eyes that you still love me, whoever I am, and you're still happy. Happy the way I used to be, before she became you.

I've only ever loved one girl and I will always love that one girl. The problem is, you aren't that girl anymore. I love the girl you used to be, and I always told you—her—that I'd do anything for her.

I hope you won't blame me for this, but it's what you told me you wanted. I remember when you said it. We were just walking out of the theater after seeing a play; a love story that ends with the girl getting her guy. You were hanging on my arm with your blue eyes wide open looking up at the stars. "If I have to die, I want to die for love," you said. I hope that much hasn't changed, because this is the only way I know how to protect the woman I love. The woman you used to be.

That first night when you became someone else, I panicked. I went into the basement to the machine I'd been building. You always called it "the Device," the capital implied by the ways you raised your eyebrows every time you said it. I didn't expect it to work. I didn't really expect it to do anything, but it did. I still can't believe it worked. The fundamental idea is sound, but it can only retrieve something from about one day in the past; just under twenty four hours. I used the machine and pulled her from your past into my present. But when I saw her start to appear I heard you start to scream upstairs so I cut it off. Is it safe to have two of you in the same time? That's where theory breaks down, and I'm not willing to take that risk. Not now, not with her at stake.

So I had the means to get her back, but that meant I had to get rid of you; I had to kill the stranger to save my wife. The first time was the hardest, believe me. You look just like her and I thought you would be gone forever. That first time, the only reason I could force myself to go through with it was because I thought she would stay. But she didn't.

That's what scares me more than...than all the rest. Every time I bring her forward, no matter what I do, you always come back. Every night I go through the same struggle to save her, knowing it will only last for a day. You always come back. It's always you. As if no matter what happens she is destined to become you at that moment. Why? What causes it? Was it a single moment that took her from me, or a thousand experiences, a million subtle decisions added together over a lifetime that bring you here each night?

It's okay though, because I've realized that I've never hurt anyone. After all, your body disappears when she materializes. Maybe when the body goes, my crime goes with it. And if I kill you every day but you come back the next, I haven't really killed you, have I?

Have I?

I'm scared too, you know. Her body stays the same age, but day by day I get older. I'm scared that one day she'll realize I've aged too much; that now I'm the one who is too different than yesterday's me to be the same person. Then she'll look at me the way you are looking at me right now, with those big blue eyes and my hand over your mouth so you can't scream.

On the day that happens, my time with her will be over and then you'll have your chance. You won't remember any of this, because it won't have ever happened to you. The world will have passed you in months or years, and I'm sorry for that, but I have to save my wife.

I'm telling you all this because I think you have a right to know why this is happening. I know you're frightened. I know you think I'm crazy. But it isn't possible for me to prove to you that everything will be okay in the end, even though it already has been. I'm sorry it has to be this way, but I love her.

It's time for me to go get her back now. Goodbye.

Oh, one last thing. I just want to say that when this is over and she and I both gone, I hope you do take those dancing lessons. If anything is true, it's this: When you find what makes you happy, you can't let anything take it away from you. Not even time itself.

THE LAST REPORT
FROM THE FRONT LINE

A bar. A fitting place, I suppose, from which to watch the heavens burn.

May I sit down? Thanks. I have a story to tell you, but there isn't much time so listen closely, okay? Bartender! Beer for the two of us here, please.

Alright then, pay attention, human: this is the story of the end of the afterlife.

I guess I should start by telling you about Wyles. In the good old days—that's what we call them, "the good old days," just like you people—Wyles and I were close friends. The best, even. Almost as close as Him and the Other used to be, before it all—half of it, I mean—went to Hell. To be honest, I still don't think that Wyles knew what he was getting into that day, but he'll never admit it. Even if he did, it really wouldn't change anything. For us, God doesn't make exceptions. Sad, isn't it? Yeah, forgiveness is a human exclusive.

Over the years, Wyles and I got into the habit of meeting up. I'll tell you why in just a second. We met at night, though we both knew that our masters could see us despite the darkness. Guess that kind of reason-less behavior should have been our first warning that we were spending too much time among you humans.

So for me to be in the city by sundown, I had to board a train this afternoon, which is where my story really starts.

When I got off the train today, it was a sunny outside with big, puffy, cotton-ball clouds skimming the tops of the city's skyline. I love trains. They're the perfect place to help put things in perspective. Trains are where I do a lot of my work, actually. The natural self-centeredness of the human mind gets introspective as the world goes by those plexiglass windows. Any stimulus, no matter how insignificant, can be imbued with miraculous properties. For instance, if I pick up the dollar you dropped and hand it back to you, that little act can, in the right circumstances, restore your faith in all of humanity. You know what I mean, little stuff like that.

By the time the train stopped, it was almost dusk and the city was falling into darkness as the sun set. From where I stood at the station, it looked like the sun was being held hostage on the horizon, trapped in a cage of oxidized iron beams that was actually just a bridge over the river. I could see the little cars on the bridge scuttling home. I like cars too. Once knew a guy who could make his whole plan of damnation just by watching how a person drove their car. He was Fallen though, and might've been lying to me.

Hmm? Oh right, you don't know what the Fallen are. Apologies, I keep forgetting this is new to you. The angels who followed Lucifer out of Heaven became demons, and we angels refer to them as Fallen most of the time. They aren't all bad, but unless you knew them in the old days, you never can tell if a Fallen is trustworthy or not.

Anyway, as I left the station I put a five in a bum's cup. He slipped it out and into a frayed pocket before the next passenger that passed by had a chance to witness the bum's good fortune. I tell you that anecdote because it represents another lesson I forgot to learn down here: always hide your strength. I didn't bother him about it though, just marched onward with a thick block of humanity around me. At the first intersection everyone else split off and I found myself alone and exposed to the city. I like trains. I like cars. I don't like cities. Too many people in them. Too easy to stop caring about each and every soul that passes you by. Souls are like snowflakes, you know: unique, but very fragile.

Even though it's late autumn, I was excited about seeing my friend again and didn't notice the cold. This jacket wasn't torn and burnt like you see it now; it was store-new then, deep blue with yellow piping along the sleeves and shoulders. As I walked it flapped a little in the gusts that hit me at every new intersection. My jeans weren't as new, but they were cleaner than you see them now.

It was about then that I sensed someone's misery nearby. I glanced down an alley and saw a human figure turn over under a newspaper, trying to get a little more comfortable on the sun-warmed concrete. I hated seeing humans like that, but I was off duty and out of my jurisdiction. I really wanted to help him, but unless something crucial to the state of his soul is happening, His Law says I can't work outside of my area. I wasn't far away from Wyles' place; if I could just focus a little more and ignore the cries for help and mercy, I could make it to his apartment early.

I stopped. I had heard something, faintly. The sound made me feel like I'd just jumped in that cold river a few blocks to my right, shoes and all. Someone hurt? Dying? Damned? I wanted to be on time to my meeting, but I just couldn't turn my back on that cry for help. Plus, this felt serious enough that the Law would allow my intervention in this case. With one lingering look towards Wyles' building, which I could just make out by then against the colors of the twilight sky, just five more blocks from across the street, I hunched my shoulders and took off at a light jog towards the west side of the city. I prayed that there was still time to help.

Turns out, there wasn't time. But I guess it really doesn't matter now, considering that—well, you'll understand when I finish my story.

I hurried back towards Wyles' place after that. He buzzed

me in and I took the stairs to the thirteenth floor since there was no elevator. The place wasn't nice enough to have numbers on the doors, but he'd told me over the intercom that he was the fourth door on the right. The carpet reeked of cat urine and weed. The door looked solid enough though, despite the wear in the varnish where too many hands had pushed it open in a hurry. I knocked, and the door behind me slid open on greased hinges; that kind of precaution going on, I should've known right then that this would be no ordinary meeting.

I didn't turn around until I heard the *thunk-tap* of his shotgun being leaned against a wall. I looked over my shoulder and saw him smiling at me, the fractured grin he'd had even before the Fall. I turned and we raised our arms as if to hug, but neither he nor I made any motion to actually embrace. Angels and demons are like antimatter; the contact of our opposite beings still isn't fully understood and we suspect that, if tried, the result would be tragic for all those involved.

"I was worried you weren't going to make it," he said.

I began to explain that I was going to arrive earlier, but he cut me off.

"Don't worry, I understand. All that matters is that you are here right now. Were you able to save the human at least?"

I shook my head.

"Pity," he replied. He meant it, too. Humans got a few things wrong with terms: demons aren't evil by definition. It was nothing more than the Choice—the day that Lucifer turned his back on Heaven—that made the Fallen the loathsome beings they are today. We call it the Choice because before that day, we angels never had an option other than to serve God. Wyles, like the rest of our species, had never had to make a choice before. The Choice happened fast though, and when it did we all had to make that decision. Like many, Wyles didn't know how to respond. He chose wrong, so now he's a demon. But he only damns enough to fill his quota so he can keep his station on earth. Or at least, that's what he told me once. I believed him.

We stepped inside his apartment. He resealed the door with two deadbolts and a prayer. Looking around, I noticed that the place had changed very little since last I had been there. It seemed as though only the security had been stepped up. Other than that, the entry room and visible living room still looked clean enough but with a hint of stuffiness, as if the windows hadn't been opened in a few months.

He pulled the blinds down over the window. "Enough business for now," he said. "Want something to drink?"

"Sure. What've you got?"

"Coke. With lemon?"

"Sounds good, Wyles. Oh, Corlissa told me to say hello and ask how you were doing."

Corlissa, I should explain, is an angel and was the third in a group of four of us that were close friends, once upon a time. The fourth? Well, you'll hear about her pretty soon too. Give me a second to get there, friend, I'm working up to dealing with her.

In Wyles' place, books sat in stacks on tables and chairs and any other flat surface in sight. I followed Wyles with my eyes around the corner and into the tiny kitchen. It was decorated in the style of the 1970's, and there were recently washed and stacked dishes by the shiny white sink. I scooped armfuls of books out of chairs so we could sit down. Wyles walked back in and set my Coke on the table near me.

"That's nice of her. I'm okay I suppose. Still damned, but what's a demon to do?"

His tone had been light, but I could see pain in his eyes over the lip of the bottle as he drank. It hurt me, too, to see my friend living like this and to know that so many others lived the same way. I didn't understand how crucial that concept of super-human empathy was for my species until later though. At the time, I just switched the topic and asked him if there was any news from Lorelei. She's the fourth one, by the way: Wyles and Corlissa, me and Lorelei.

"Actually, yeah. She's been promoted and is working on something official. I forget what she called it last time we spoke. It's been a few weeks." He looked at the windows with worry in his eyes even though the blinds stopped us from seeing outside. "Lots of activity lately, Brody."

Something in his tone disturbed me, and I tried probing further. I tried to sound casual when I asked him if he knew what was happening.

He heard the change in my voice though, smiled, and let his pointed teeth show through his disguise. "Brody, Brody, Brody. Never forget that I'm not on your side anymore. You and I are old friends, and we've both got people that we still care about who were separated by this war. But we're just foot soldiers, Brody; we can afford to meet over the front line like this. The generals and the admirals can't. This is their war. I may be Fallen, but the Devil's men have virtue too, and I'm loyal to my master. You won't learn more from me than you already know." He turned his eyes toward the wall, and when he looked back again he had recovered his composure as well as his disguise.

My cheeks were hot. "I'm sorry, Wyles, I shouldn't have asked that. You've always respected the neutrality of our meetings." I squeezed another lemon slice into my Coke and sipped without meeting his eyes.

But I could sense that he was studying me. "It's all well and done, old friend. Perhaps I took it more seriously than I should have." He smiled disarmingly. "Let's not ruin this reunion so quickly, hmm? You've got the normal shipment, don't you?"

I moved my shabby old briefcase from the floor to the tabletop. Wyles didn't even blink, didn't even open it when he pulled it across the table. He trusted me. How could he not? I am an angel after all; swindling isn't something my kind is known for.

"Thank you," was all he said. But I knew he was grateful.

Curious what was in the briefcase? Of course you are, you're human. Truth is that it was another near miss of your mythology: ambrosia. You heard me right. Food of the gods and all that, except that it's actually for angels. It's good stuff, really. Think of it this way; after living on ambrosia, eating anything without it is kind of like switching to skim milk from whole; you always feel like the real food is missing. Angelic creatures can technically "eat" anything on earth, but we are only nourished by ambrosia, and ambrosia can, of course, only be found in Heaven. Naturally the once-angelic don't have access to it once they are Fallen. But they can't die from starvation, either. This denial of sustenance is just another eternal punishment for them, albeit an unintended one. Watching such cruel punishment meted out to our friends is unbearable for us angels; after all, our sole purpose here is to relieve suffering.

And that's why Wyles and I risk meeting every month. Friends on my side of the Buffer send me what they can along with names for it to go to. We aren't hiding this operation, but we aren't advertising either. The stuff funnels in to me from all across the Kingdom, and I take it into the Buffer—that is, earth, the world of both good and evil that separates Hell from Heaven—and pass it on. On the other side it gets passed out. I assume it goes to the right people, but I don't really know. I know my part goes to Lorelei though; Wyles wouldn't cheat me that.

I used to get letters from her, gushing with thanks. That stopped long, long ago. Sounds like she was doing well for herself though. I had my own theories of why she stopped writing to me but I guess after today, none of that matters anymore. For centuries I'd sent her what I could, even when she became Sixth Temptress. Now I don't even know what her rank is, since I can't find out, she stopped writing, and Wyles never told.

Speaking of the devil, Wyles' phone had rung about then and he had gone to answer it in the other room. I sat, enjoyed my Coke, and heard only muffled, emphatic talk. After my earlier rebuffing though, I didn't want to listen in and piss Wyles off again.

Come to think of it, this day might've ended a lot differently if I had listened to that conversation; I might actually know who to believe.

Regardless, he came back in the room, took his seat, grabbed his bottle, and just sat and looked at the closed window blinds. That's when I really started getting worried. He's usually much more talkative than this. Something was going on, but I was afraid to ask him what it was.

I stood up at that point, awkwardly resettling my jacket on my shoulders. By then I'd been there fifteen or twenty minutes. This was when I usually left. "Hey, Wyles, I think I should get going. It was good seeing you." It didn't even look like he had heard me. "Hey man, I'm heading out."

He still didn't respond, so I turned my back to him and headed for the door.

"That was her, Brody."

The doorknob suddenly felt very cold in my hand.

"She's coming to see you."

I took a step back into the room. He was still staring at the window even though he couldn't see outside. I knew who he was talking about, but at that time I didn't know why it disturbed him so badly. I would've been happy to see her again in any other circumstance, but Wyles' obvious fear gave me pause.

I matched his serious tone. "I thought she couldn't leave Hell without permission. What is she doing in the Buffer, Wyles?"

That's when he looked at me at last. He stood up and turned around and looked me square in the eye. He'd dropped his disguise entirely, and for the first time ever I saw his full demonic figure.

"Brody, I'm sorry. It's like I said before: we're just foot soldiers. This whole thing is much bigger than us. We just do the best we can, right?"

That next moment still seems like it took too long to have happened so fast. I was about to ask him what he was talking about when the wall behind me exploded. Next thing I knew,

Wyles had twin streams of smoking black ichor oozing out of bullet holes in his scale-covered chest and I was on my knees on the floor.

I brushed plaster dust out of my hair and looked up. She had a pistol in her hand and her tail was lashing back and forth in the hallway behind her where the door used to be. Even as a demon she was beautiful.

"It's good to see you, Broden," she said.

I looked from Lorelei back towards Wyles' spiritless body. The black spines protruding from his back in his true form had caught on the window blinds and as he fell the blinds had been ripped from their mountings. I could see out the windows now. Outside, the city's skyline was visible against red clouds that burned on the horizon despite the night. Until that moment alone, I had not known fear.

"Lorelei, what's going on?" I asked her. I won't deny that the words trembled as they left my throat.

Hell hounds barked from down the hall, heading straight for us.

"I'm sorry, but I don't have time to explain, Broden. You see the clouds. You know what is happening. Wyles betrayed you, kept you distracted here while the plan went into effect. I came as quickly as I could to stop him. His orders were to keep you from your duties, to stop you from warning Heaven that Hell's forces were mobilizing. Broden, he was ordered to kill you."

I was on my feet now and just starting to actually process everything she had told me.

"Then those hounds are coming for you, aren't they?"

"Yes, but I'm not afraid. Good-bye, Broden. Forgive me."

And then she kissed me.

She was gone the moment her lips touched mine. Not dead—we can't "die"—but annihilated. Lost forever to oblivion. Like I said before, demons and angels aren't supposed to touch. To be honest, I'm still not sure why the same thing didn't happen to me. The hounds, sent out to punish her for the sin of killing a fellow demon, fled back to

Hell now that there was no one to bring back. And there I was, alone with the shell of my best friend lying on the floor beside me and the burning of a demon's kiss on my lips.

I tell you, I started to go up to Heaven to sound the alarm, hoping there was still time to assemble the Host for the Final Battle prophesized by scripture.

But I didn't do it.

I stopped, and I came back down to the Buffer. I came back because I thought that at least a few humans should know what is happening. And to be honest, this is where I want to be at the end of days. Pubs have always been the antithesis of my work; you don't think about the world in a bar, you escape from it. And that's exactly what I want right now.

As angels, we were all happy because we were all one. But then came the Choice, and we were divided. I can't help thinking that it wasn't the side that you picked that was important in the end, just the fact that there was a choice at all that ruined us. We aren't like you humans; we weren't designed to make decisions.

You must understand that we were born with everything we could want, and no desire for anything else. It wasn't until the advent of the Great Divorce that we began to learn of loss. All of us, even the angels, suffer now in our own way. For a human, empathy means to imagine what another feels. For an angel, empathy means to actually *feel* what another feels. We all have friends in Hell, and we see their pain and there is nothing we can do about it. The prophecies talk of the great battle, but we live with its outcome even before the battle has happened: somehow, we've all already lost. It took me until now to realize that.

My closest friends, demons both, are gone and I don't know what to believe. Too many questions are left. If Wyles were going to kill me, why didn't he? Why was he so shaken to hear that Lorelei was coming? How did she get out of Hell?

From what Lorelei told me, the plan was to have Wyles kill me so that Hell could make its move before Heaven knew what was happening. Makes sense I guess. Some demon must've figured out that I was the highest ranking angel down here. But Lorelei found out about the plan, sacrificed herself to find me first and stop Wyles from following his orders. Knowing what would happen to her, she decided to end it on her own terms, and to touch me one more time.

Of course, I never got the sense that Wyles was actually trying to kill me. That means there is another possibility: maybe those were his orders, but he couldn't go through with it. Maybe Lorelei was given permission to leave Hell to make sure the plan wasn't ruined, slayed Wyles for his disobedience or so he didn't get in her way, and kissed me. Why the kiss then? Maybe she thought it would annihilate me too.

But it didn't. So what did it do?

As I sit here talking it out with you, I'm beginning to suspect that I didn't survive her touch intact. Maybe she left part of herself on me. That could be the source of these thoughts. Either she knew what would happen if an angel and a demon touched, and desired it, and included me in it, or she didn't know and hoped it would destroy both of us. Maybe the mix of angel and demon has given me a taste of what it is like to be human, to see both right and wrong and be damned to indecision and insecurity because of that dual sight.

Or maybe I've just spent too much time in the Buffer.

Truth is, I don't know. And I don't want to know. I don't care if this was their plan all along or not. I want everything to be done, and I think all of us angelic beings will be happier with it that way; no more separation, no more choices. How do you people live like this, day in and day out?

And that's what it all comes down to, isn't it. You humans were made with forgiveness and grace, and we angels were not.

We don't have any place to go, but we don't need one. We've all been to Heaven and lost it, one way or the other. We're separated now, and the only way to be united again is in oblivion.

So that's why I'm here, telling you this story. I thought at least one of you should hear it anyway. Don't believe me? Look outside and see for yourself. Look at the heavens, see them burn. That's the end of the afterlife, my friend. No more Heaven; no more Hell.

Why?

Well because at this point, the Big Guy can't win this fight. But here's another thing you probably didn't know since we've gone out of our way to keep it a secret from you humans: the rules He wrote don't say that good always prevails, they say that evil always loses. It's a small difference, but an important one. As soon as the Other takes the Throne, it's lights out for all of us celestials. Otherwise, why would it be so important that I be down here standing guard, ready to sound the alarm?

For me and my kind, that's alright. It's our escape. We can finally be freed from the torment we weren't designed to endure; we can be free from this separation. We can be one again.

What's going to happen to you? I wish I could say. It's possible the Buffer will survive and you'll all live out your lives just the same, but without us agents interfering all the time. What should you do? Nothing you can do, friend, so don't worry about it. Have a pint. Do your best with the gifts you've been given. That's all the advice I can offer.

Now let's finish our drinks, for I feel my time here is spent. This one I raise to Corlissa, whose innocence I have made the choice to protect so that she wouldn't have to. Don't remember her? Good; that's the point. May she continue to be free from choice, forever and ever.

Amen.

THE DEFINITION

Earnest T. Chenkowitz is a man of order.

Anyone would tell you so. Ask his colleagues at Yale. Put the question to his barber, who trims Chenky's hair at two o'clock every Sunday afternoon. Ask either of his daughters, Amelia or Cynthia.

Well, perhaps not Amelia. She had been the one who had had him committed.

Seven o'clock in the morning: Dr. Chenkowitz rises from his bed, showers, and brushes his teeth. He reads fiction until eight, at which point he and the other guests are invited to breakfast.

Amelia had been the one to sign the papers anyway. Earnest knows it had been all three of them—the others were complicit, if not involved. Cynthia didn't have the stomach to put her own father away, but she was a good girl; she always listened to her mother. He remembered how much his wife Beth had cried that time she came to visit. That had been about two years ago now.

Shakespeare's Lear, Cervantes' Quixote, and Chenkowitz. A long, proud line of men abused by ungrateful family.

He should have done more research, been better prepared before he represented himself in court, he knows that now. He

43

knows so many things now that he has time to think about them. Brilliance is often taken for insanity. If you want to be happy, it's best to be born in the fat womb of the bell-shaped curve. Society doesn't like extremes.

Eleven o'clock: morning constitutional in the yard. The path is so worn down along the fence, it shows as a sustained indentation despite the inches of snow on the ground. Dutifully, Dr. Chenkowitz plows ahead, his mind so consumed by his latest work that he stops short when he realizes that, for the first time in months, the skies are clear blue and the sun is shining over the snow-powdered roof of St. Abraham's Care Facility for the Disturbed. One lap. Two laps. Three. A horn sounds from the tallest guard tower.

Twelve o'clock: Earnest retreats to the library to work. Harriet is sitting in a steel chair near the entrance, her feet wrapped around its legs, pushing it back against the wall.

"Good day, Dr. Chenkowitz!" Harriet says. She is smiling up from behind her book. "It's today, isn't it? Today's the day!"

Earnest ignores her. He goes to the brightest seat in the library, where the tall thin windows let in the afternoon sun in long, unbroken banners. He hangs his sport coat over the back of the chair at the grey table. Referring to a paper from his briefcase, he goes back into the legal section of the institution's library. All of the books are filmed in dust. All of them except one. Earnest spends three minutes finding the next book on his list. He brings the volume down carefully with both hands. Returning to his table, Earnest places the book before him and runs a pale hand across the old leather. The edges of the pages are trimmed in gold, like a Bible, or like a paper plate at a child's birthday party. Earnest flips open the book and begins to read. Across the room, Harriet looks up from her novel. She whispers to herself, "Today's the day! Today's the day!"

One o'clock: Earnest slams the book shut in frustration and raises it over his head. He is going to throw it. He is going to send it flying through the narrow windows and out into the snow. He is going to—looking up, he spies Harriet watching him. Her eyes are big and yellow, like the pages of the paperback in her hands. Earnest lowers the book to the table and lets out a long sigh. Anger will do him no good here. Anger will only feed the psychologist's theories and prove his family's suppositions. What he needs to find is peace.

And that damned definition.

Earnest forces a smile in Harriet's direction. She cowers behind the thin armor of her paperback. Earnest eases the legal book open and resumes reading where he had left off.

At four o'clock an orderly comes to inform Chenkowitz that his presence is requested at a meeting. Unusual. Chenkowitz obliges the young man, but insists on bringing the book he is currently reading.

"No can do, sir," the orderly tells him. "But don't you worry, it'll be here tomorrow when you come back for it, just like always."

Chenkowitz allows himself to be escorted from the library to the conference room. The room is painted in pale, horizontal shades of blue and grey. Two men and a woman sit in a row behind a steel table. The panel of doctors greet him and ask him how he is feeling.

"Stupendous. Terrific. Now if you'll excuse me, I must continue my work."

The doctor at the end of the table smiles. "What are you working on, Dr. Chenkowitz?"

Chenkowitz glares. "You know damn well what I'm working on, Dr. Erstein. I'm trying to get out of here."

"How?"

Chenkowitz's hand twitches, missing the weight of the legal book, the feel of the old leather. "Society has defined me as insane. I know that I am not. Therefore, to prove that I am not, I must find the proper definition to show this. If I can just find the definition—"

"But you did find it, Dr." the woman says, putting a hand on the arm of the man beside her to quiet him. "You read it out loud, in court. Dr. Briggs was there." The man on her opposite side nods his head. "And your family—"

"It obviously was not the right one," Chenkowitz snarls,

"because I am still here, aren't I! No, law is a fickle beast. There are hundreds of definitions of insanity, thousands of variations. If I can only find the proper one, you will have to let me get back to my life, back to my real work!"

With that, Chenkowitz storms from the room. They don't try to stop him. Dr. Erstein chuckles before a glare from Dr. Briggs cuts him off. Dr. Briggs puts a comforting hand on the woman's shoulder beside him.

"How are you doing, Cynthia?" he asks her.

She shakes her head. She's crying. "He doesn't even recognize me anymore. He doesn't even recognize his own daughter."

Briggs rubs her back. "He's getting worse. I'm sorry."

Cynthia stands and gathers her things. "You're right. I know you're right." She wipes her eyes. "Thank you for your time, doctors. Shall we meet again next week?"

Briggs and Erstein look at each other. "Uh, sure thing, Ms. Chenkowitz. We'll see you then," Briggs answers. Cynthia walks out of the room, the curls of her hair bouncing against her shoulders with each step.

Joel Erstein says, "Why do we keep doing this, Sam? You said yourself that he's getting worse. Why do you let her keep coming in here and torturing herself like this?"

"What happened to your milk of human kindness, Joel? She wants to see her dad. And we are supposed to be helping these people, not just guarding them. Remember?"

"Sure, I remember that." Joel wipes his glasses on his shirt. "But the state doesn't pay us for how many we help, it pays us for how many we hold. You remember *that*, alright?" He stands up and straightens his shirt.

"I've never forgotten it."

"Good."

Joel stalks towards the door into the hall. He turns back and looks at Dr. Briggs. "I'm not coming to these things anymore, Sam. I'm too busy, and she's too ugly when she cries."

"That's fine, Joel."

* * *

Sam Briggs steps into his office just in time to hear his phone ringing.

"Sam? It's Amelia. How did it go today?"

"Well, you know how these things are—"

"Don't toy with me, Sam, you've got money on this. How close is she to breaking?"

"It's definitely getting to her, just like we got to him. But she's tougher than he was. It's just going to take some time, Ms. Chenkowitz."

"I hate when you call me that."

"I know you do."

The line is silent. Then, quietly, she says, "I never expected this. I mean, I thought once we put daddy away, that would be the end of it and we'd get the money. But that didn't happen. There was more to do; we had to do it over again. Once you get Cynthia, that's it, right? It'll be over?" Amelia sounds frightened. She is looking to *him* for strength. It makes him want to laugh.

"That'll be it, Amelia. I promise," he tells her instead.

After another long silence Amelia says, "Sam, are we doing the right thing?"

Sam shrugs. "What's the definition of insanity?"

"Fuck you, Sam."

The line goes dead. Sam replaces the receiver and leans back in his chair. He can't stop smiling. In just a few weeks, he will have broken Cynthia. That's good. That means he is ahead of schedule. Next time they talked, he'd have to remember to ask Amelia how her mom was holding up under the stress...

I LOVED YOU ONCE AND FOREVER
-a binary tale of love and identity-

I LOVED YOU ONCE, TOO

Look at me.

I read your note. I read about what you did each day, why you did it. You were scared—I read that in your note, too. Scared because this day had come and you couldn't face it, even though you'd known today was coming since way back. And you were sorry, you said, so sorry for 'what you had to do.'

What did you expect from me, sympathy? Understanding?

Maybe that's what 'she' would've given you, but not me. If you weren't right before, you are now: I'm not the woman you used to love. Hell, I'm not even the woman you fell *out* of love with anymore. She's long gone. I'm someone else— someone neither of us has met before.

Have you realized what today is yet? Yes, I can see in the shape of your eyes and the slouch of your shoulders that you have. I won. Finally, after all these times, I got away. Today's the day we switched places. Today's the day you weren't you anymore.

There was a man too old to be my husband, so I ran. But it wasn't safe outside either. A nightmare world out there. I recognized some of the parts, but it was as if someone had reassembled them wrong. I don't know how long I wandered out there. It must've been a few hours. The bank was where it always was, downtown, squatting between storefronts I couldn't recollect seeing before. That's where I saw the calendar.

It's been almost four years since yesterday. At least, for me it has been. 'Coma' was my first thought; it was the easiest answer. So I'd overreacted, right? I took a breath, calmed down, and came home.

I walked in the door and found you here, slumped over your desk with a bullet in your brain. When I finished reading your letter a second time, your ranting was starting to be more plausible. I mean, they don't keep coma patients at home.

So I read your letter and I went down to the basement. You were telling the truth. I can't believe it either, but it worked. Just like you said it would.

But you messed up. You were too eager. So now you're here. Again.

Don't look away, look at *me*.

You'll be here again and again and again until *I* decide we're even, until *I* say that I'm satisfied.

I want you to understand what's going to happen now. I'm going to murder you. Then I'm going to use your own device to get you back. We're going to walk up here slowly, hand in hand. You'll be so happy to see 'me' again. When we get to the living room, you'll turn to me and I'll smile like *this*, and the knife will enter you like *this*, and you'll sink to the floor. I'll give you this speech while you die, like now, and I'll watch as the horror spreads in your eyes and you realize that you'll never get to join 'her.'

You may have been doing it to save her, but you were hurting me. You were selfish, all your reasons were selfish. Now I get to be selfish, to make myself feel better at your expense. I get to do this for me—for all of me. Goodbye.

* * *

Stop struggling. Those straps are too strong. Just let me talk.

One was enough. I know how it feels now, and I'm sorry. You weren't right, but…you weren't wrong, either.

It was all true. You're sitting there again, just like yesterday, and you don't even know what I'm talking about, because yesterday never happened to you. You don't remember when I stabbed you, when I killed you.

But there's more than just that. You were telling the truth about that moment, too. I saw it on your face when I brought you back today.

Yesterday, even as I killed you, you were still in love with me. The moment hadn't passed yet. But for the first time in four years, I survived last night and something in me changed. Not you, because you've gone back. So it must have happened to *me*. This time, today, your love was gone and I knew it the moment you looked at me. You never lied. You really did it for us—for love.

Look at me. Please.

This isn't easy for me, but I can't hold what you did against you. It's just not in me, now that I understand what you went through. I think I feel the same way you felt every night, trying to hold on but watching me—her—get further away. Knowing what I know now, I can't hold on to my anger. I don't want revenge anymore.

And I think I still love you, whoever you are.

We're different people now, there's no denying that. But you never looked far enough ahead: in time we'll be different people yet. So I've still got hope for us. Maybe, someday, our moments will converge again. I can hope for that.

It won't be easy—it'll be the hardest thing I've ever done—but I can wait. For you, I would wait forever. And thanks to you, I can. I can bring you back over and over, until the day comes when your eyes open and you look at me and

I'll know it was worth it because whoever you are will love whoever I am.

I'm sorry for what I've done and for what I have to do. But I know that this is what he'll want, whenever you're him— what *we'll* want, whenever we're them.

IN SICKNESS AND IN HELL

There was a knock at the front door like a polite cough. I pushed myself up from the kitchen table to answer it but my mind stayed where it had been ever since I got off the phone with the doc. That was two hours ago. I couldn't stop myself thinking today, going over all our problems in my head. Worrying, like I knew something big was going on but I couldn't figure out what.

I passed the bedroom and I glanced in but Dawn was twisted up under the covers like her stomach was hurting, so I left her alone.

Things had been bad between us for a coupla weeks. We wasn't sleeping together lately, and we'd been fighting more than I remembered ever doing in the past. I don't know what came first, but I think one musta caused the other. Goddamn chickens and eggs, you follow?

Anyway, even with that shit going on I was pretty sure I still believed in *us*. I still wanted to marry the girl. Green eyes, slim body, and a laugh like an angel, who wouldn't? And I still had a strong notion that if I was dumb enough to ask, she'd agree to it. I had already went and talked with her dad about it all, real formal-like to settle things between men. Invited him out to dinner—which for us is rare—and when the check came

I offered to pay—which for me is unheard of. Did all that just so I wouldn't have to surprise him with the idea; before he ordered dessert, he knew the stakes.

I really had no reason to be worried though, and we both knew it. It's a fuckin' dance now, a bit a American culture, like buying a cake for your cat's birthday even though she's diabetic. You're not gonna get a sugar free cake for the animal though, am I right? It's not like you're actually gonna feed it the cake, it's just something people do.

Anyway, my point is that things was all set, everything in place, but I still didn't pop the big Q. Dawn gave me some strong hints that she was ready, even mentioned it once or twice while we were heels to heaven—that pissed me off—but I still didn't get around to it. It was just never the right time, you know?

So like I started with, it's been bad for a few weeks between her and me. I got the flu or some shit and that's when I started sleeping on the couch, so I wouldn't infect her. But when I got better it wasn't the same between us. Don't know if it was me or her or both of us, but that's what happened. I'd say that's when we stopped sleeping together for real, not because I was sick anymore. We've lived together for a couple years now, and I know I can get pretty irritating, so it wasn't the first time I'd crashed in the living room because she didn't want me too close. I was used to it. Hell, when we found the couch, I knew there'd be more than a chance's last nickel I'd be sleeping on it now and again.

But Dawn got sick not long after I started feeling better anyway. She's sick now, been sick for weeks, much worse'n I ever was. Maybe that's why she didn't want me around her, 'cause she was feeling bad. Could be.

I'm still gonna ask her, just as soon as she gets better. I can't ask her now, Dawn'd kill me if I went in there and said "Marry me, beautiful?" when she's still nauseous, bed-ridden, and got hair like Haiti inna hurricane.

It's gonna be alright though. Something tells me it will be. A buddy I met at work told me yesterday about this doctor he knew that did house calls. Dawn's a receptionist and I'm a part-timer at a lumber yard, so we don't make all that much money. John, the owner, says he might be able to hire me full-time in a few months, but I'll believe it when the check clears. He's a sack a shit anyway.

So Franks—that's what we call the new forklift operator 'cause he smells like hot dogs—overheard me telling one a the guys that Dawn wasn't feeling so great. He gave me the number for this Dr. Mayline and told me he's real good and understands people like us that can't afford to go to the doctor's or the emergency room. I gave the Doc a call early today and he said he'd be over in a few hours to see her.

Before I opened the front door, I checked the peephole. In the clean, bright daylight outside—I had all the shades drawn in the house—there was a fat looking, almost geeky-faced guy in tan slacks and a button down. His ears stuck out from his head like a bull's horns. I wondered why he didn't wear a hat or something.

I swung the door open. He gave me the once over, looked bothered by what he saw, covered it up with a weak smile and stumbled over an introduction.

"Sam? Hi, I'm Dr. Mayline. Can I come in?"

"'Course, Doc. Nice to meet you," I said, extending my hand. He glanced down at it nervously.

"Sorry," he explained, "germs."

"Ah, right, sorry," I wiped my hand on my shirt. I almost felt offended, but then I thought he's a doctor, he knows best. "This way, come on in." I led him down the hall, and we sat down in the kitchen. He was carrying a big black leather bag, like the ones old-time doctors with those shiny discs on their heads mighta carried if they did house calls. Come to think of it, I don't know if ones like them did house calls or not...

"Where's the, ah, patient?" the doc asked.

"Oh, Dawn's in the bedroom, through there," I said, pointing at a bead curtain doorway that led across the hall. Doctor Mayline was sitting at the chrome-edged table with his big bag in his lap. He was looking around at the décor. It made me a little embarrassed, because it was all black and white tiles with red accents and lots of chrome. Dawn had thought that a 50's diner look would be cute for the kitchen, and I had figured that we didn't have people over much anyway so who cares if it looks ridiculous, so long as the girl's happy. It mighta been one of those things where we did it and then both pretended to like it just so we wouldn't have to do it again. I'm not sure. I offered the doc a drink.

He shifted in his red and white v-back diner chair—we got the set off a E-bay for cheap—and looked uncomfortable.

"Sam, sorry, but I am very busy. Would you mind going and finding out if Dawn is ready to see me yet?"

"Huh? Oh, sure, hold on a minute," I said, feeling like a retard. Of course he wants to see Dawn. I went into our room. The shades were down in here too and there was an acidy smell in the air.

"You throw up again, honey?" I asked. I heard her moan out a yes. "Well don't you worry, the doctor's here to see you." She took a couple deep, slow breaths. It sounded like they hurt. The white sheets rustled and she pulled herself upright, propping herself up on her arms.

She looked like hell. I knew she'd had trouble sleeping the last coupla nights, and there was dark circles under her eyes for proof. Her hair had gone wiry and wild; strands of it either stuck up randomly around her head or else hung limp against her pale shoulders.

Dawn tried a smile but it came out more a grimace. "Hey there, handsome. Mind getting a girl a shirt?" she asked me. She was clutching the blankets to her breasts as if she was cold, but lines of her dark hair was plastered against her face, like a cross section of a coal mine.

I tossed a t-shirt on the bed beside her. She pulled it over her head, using both hands to draw her hair out of the neck in a big, static-y mass.

"Shit," she said, "Sam, I don't want *you* to see me like this, much less a stranger."

I said, "I know, but he's gonna help, trust me. You'll feel

better soon." I sat on the bed beside her and pushed some of the hair off of her face. It wasn't just the hair around her face, her whole body was soaked in cold sweat. I tried to kiss her but she put a hand on my chest and turned away. "Get the doctor, Sam. Please." She pulled the covers up to her neck again. "And empty the puke pot, too. Thanks, babe."

When either of us was sick, we'd use our big silver soup pot to puke in. I found it next to the bed and I saw where she hadn't gotten all of it into the pot. There was a brownish-red trail dripping down the edge of the mattress. It smelled like fried crap, and I carried the pot outta the room at arm's length.

I was feeling scared. Seeing Dawn like that reminded me of my momma before she died. I've never seen anyone look that way that wasn't fighting for their life against something.

Doc Mayline looked up at me anxiously when I pushed through the hanging beads into the kitchen again.

"Is she ready?" he asked. I said yea and he got to his feet and told me to stay in the kitchen and wait while he examined her. "It's very important that I am not interrupted. I'll get you if I need you, okay Sam?"

"Yeah, sure thing, Doc, just call."

He went in and I heard him introduce himself to Dawn and then he shut the door behind him and I couldn't hear any more. I was alone in the kitchen. It seemed kinda weird that I couldn't be in there with him, but I didn't move to contradict him or nothing. I just sat for a few minutes, worrying, watching the strings of beads swing back and forth over the door frame like the pendulums of a hundred grandfather clocks, all outta sync.

There was another knock at the door. I wasn't expecting nobody and I didn't think that Dawn was either. There was a chance it was some a her friends, but honestly that lot wasn't the type to drop in with a cup a soup to cheer you up.

I checked the peephole again—kind of a habit of mine, it's not like I'm ever expecting *not* to open the door, but it's there so I figure why not use it?—and saw two men on my front step. They looked pretty normal: not dressed up much, just jeans, t-shirts, and jackets so I figured they wasn't selling anything and they wasn't proslatizing. I opened the door a crack.

"Hello, sir," the man in front said warily, "does a Dawn Orlens live—holy shit, Carpenter? Is that you, man?"

I looked him over again. He had a thin beard that clung to the underside of his jawline like moss on a rock and strong creases under his eyes that swept diagonally down from the sides of his stubby nose. He looked a little familiar, like a guy that I used to skip class with in grade school. But that guy had been a jackass and a burnout, and I think it was in the paper that he tried to kill himself a while back. Cut his wrists. Messy shit.

The front man removed his hat, apparently thinking that that would help my memory. "Carpenter," he said, "fucksticks, man, you don't recognize me? We used to hang all the time outside of school!" He held out his hand for a handshake like as if he was an old friend. Looking down, I saw the scars on the inside of his wrist. Crossed the tracks. Dumbshit didn't even take the time to fuckin' hari kari his shit right.

That was enough to convince me that yeah, this was Andrew Birmham alright. But he looked so different; world-weary, like something was eating at him. And who knows, maybe that's how I look to him, too. But who the hell was this other prick? And what the hell was they doing on my stoop? And what the fuck did they want with Dawn?

I asked them those same questions in those same words.

Dawn's name musta snapped them outta the moment 'cause the other guy jabbed Andy in the shoulder like what-gives-man-we-got-a-job-to-do, and Andy let go of my hand and asked if they could come inside.

When I told them that Dawn was sick, they nodded like they was expecting to hear that. When I said that the doctor was with her, they flipped their shit.

They both started talking at once: "Carpenter, you've got to let us in *right now* or it'll be too late for her," Andy said in a violent whisper while his buddy asked, "How long has it been alone with her?"

I said, "Fuck if I know, five minutes? What's going—"

"Let us in, Carpenter!" Andy hissed. His eyes was looking over my shoulder like he thought someone other than me was gonna hear him.

Something in my head told me I shouldn't, but I ignored it and invited them into the house. I got pushed against the wall in their rush to get inside and the front door got slammed into my shoulder.

"Where is the bastard?" Andy's friend said, his burning eyes grazing me as he scanned the dirty living room for someone he musta hated, 'cause you don't get that crazy look in your eyes about someone you don't know. He reached inside his jacket and pulled a goddamn silver cane of a revolver out of it.

"Whoa, man, what's the prob—" I began, but Andy cut me off:

"Carpenter!" He grabbed me by the shirt front and shook me. "That's not a doctor! That's why we're here!"

My eyes snapped to the bedroom door; down the hall to my left, at right angles to the kitchen. Following my eyes, the second man crossed the living room and was down the hall before I could speak.

He didn't try the door knob, just used some sorta kung-fuckin'-fu kick to break the door free. I saw him bringing the gun down level as his momentum carried him forward into the room.

From where I was standing, too shocked to swear, still with my shirt in Andy's fist, I watched the pistol's Coke-can of a cylinder rotate in slow motion.

I was all kinds of hopped up on adrenaline now, I could tell; everything around me was moving slow, like a bad trip where you start thinking *fuck, man, this is it, this is it,* and you wanna just crash. You start watching the clock but the hands are pointing at you and laughing, and you're going nuts inside your head because you just want to cover your eyes and make everything go away but your arms are made of goddamn lead.

My eyes hadn't moved yet. I hadn't moved yet. I watched the hammer rear back. Then, at last, a single thought lit up my brain like lightning over a lake:

Dawn's gonna fuckin' die.

I didn't doubt what Andy or his butcherous buddy had told me, didn't stop to think about how little I knew of what was going on. I was in way over my head—I musta been aware of that somewhere in the back of my skull—but there wasn't nothing as important to me right now as the sick girl in the bedroom.

I shoved Andy back and ran down the hallway, bouncing off the walls, my arms flailing, trying to stay balanced. Picture frames crashed to the ground around me, knocked off their nails. I heard the frames strike the tiles and the glass inside shatter, coating the floor. Andy was on my heels, crunching up the glass fragments almost as fast as I could make 'em. Ahead of me, the trigger clicked into place and I saw the hammer strike home.

The entire house shuddered. Dust jumped off the walls and hung in the air. Forget bullets, the ball of fire that came outta the end of that pistol hadta've fried the perv, I thought. But no, now Andy's friend was going into the room, and his trigger finger was already tensing for round two.

My right shoulder was still throbbing from when Andy had slammed the front door into me, so I really felt it when I hit the shattered door frame in my rush to reach Dawn.

I got just one peek inside before Andy caught up with me in a flying tackle that sent us both crashing through the bead curtain and into the kitchen.

That one look was just enough to remind me that I had no idea what the hell was happening in my cramped little house.

The sheets had been thrown on the floor beside the bed, along with the t-shirt I had given Dawn justa few minutes ago. She was on the bed, naked and unmoving, her green eyes unnaturally wide. And there were things placed around and on her body; creepy looking crap that I didn't getta good enough look at to describe. The doc musta been standing over her on the bed when he was interrupted, 'cause by the time I saw him his body was in free fall, just about to make contact with the carpet on the far side of the room. Since I had last seen him, Doc Mayline had gained two holes the size of my fists through his chest. Going by the oval-shaped splatters of gore on the wall, the slugs had picked him up and thrown him before they punched all the way through.

Damn.

Andy and I landed in a heap, him on top, on the black and white laminate. I started yelling for Dawn: "Baby, can you hear me? You okay? I'm coming to help you, babe, just hold on!"

"Sam!" Andy was yelling at me. He was braced over me, his hands placed just below my biceps so I couldn't get any leverage on him. I kept trying to throw him off anyway. I could feel the strain in every tendon of my body as I tried to twist out of his grip. "Sam, control yourself, man! It's alright, Thomas'll finish him. That's why we're here. That's what we do, man!"

It didn't matter what he was saying, I was beyond words now. I wanted to destroy anything that stood between me and making sure Dawn was okay. Especially Andy and this other guy. I woulda killed Andy right then and there—was trying to, really—but he outweighed me by thirty and already had me pinned.

From the bedroom I heard a sudden inhalation of air, like as if someone was drowning and had just broken into the sunlight again.

Then the breath cut off, and I heard Dawn's voice begin to scream. Her voice, but somehow I knew it wasn't Dawn. Something else was using her voice, and it was pissed off beyond all reason.

I started yelling again too, because I felt the same way. I was hoping that Dawn could hear me, hoping she would understand that I was still fighting, that I hadn't abandoned her.

"Andy!" the man named Thomas called from the bedroom, "I need some help in here! This demon is fucking *strong!*"

"Damn it!" Andy spat, still fighting to keep me on my back. "I'm coming, hold on, Tom!" Andy looked down at me. "Sorry, man, but this is for your own good. We can't let you in there until she's stable." He let go of my right arm just long enough to grab me by the hair and slam the back of my head into the floor.

I've been knocked out before, but this time it didn't go dark.

I don't know if it's even possible to dream while unconscious, but I did. I was still on the floor, still lying there staring at the cobwebs and fingerprints on the underside of our kitchen table, and I could hear everything that was going on in the other room: snarling, yelling, moaning, and the wet sound of soft flesh and sharp steel. But I couldn't move. And I was being crushed by this feeling of guilt like I've never felt before, because it was me that let them all inside. That was important, I knew it was, but I couldn't figure out why. And now I was just lying here, doing nothing while Dawn was in danger. There was more: I became aware that it was *all* my fault. Not just today, but the fights and the flu and all the rest. I had done this. I had made all of this happen. But I still didn't know what the fuck "all of this" was.

When I came to, Thomas was kneeling at my left side, looking at my eyes with a worried expression. His face shifted just slightly towards relief when I moved my eyes to look at him. His hand relaxed its grip on that goliath pistol. It hadn't been pointed at me, but it also hadn't *not* been pointed at me, you follow? Someone had put an ice pack under my head like a pillow. I started to struggle to my feet but Thomas put a hand on my shoulder and pushed me back down. "Whoa, there, take a second and collect yourself," he told me. I was too weak to do anything but take his advice.

My mind started seeing details again. I saw that Tom's clothing was singed and his hair looked dry and frail. His goatee and eyebrows were burnt too.

"Dawn," I said.

"She's okay," he assured me, "for now. But she's not out of danger yet."

"The Doc?"

"That host is dead. We cut off all of its senses." Tom smiled cruelly. "You don't need to worry about him anymore." Tom's face turned grave. "But we need you on your feet, Sam. We need your help if we're going to save Dawn. Have you got yourself under control?"

I said, "Yeah, yeah I'm fine. Help me up. Where's Andy?"

"He's still in there with her. We've got her stable, but we can't get that bastard out of her without you."

I didn't waste my breath asking what that was supposed to mean. I tried to take a step towards the bedroom and stumbled. Tom caught me under the arms and held me up. "Sam, I know that this is all happening fast for you, but you have to trust us for the next couple of minutes, okay? Andy and I need you to go in there and talk to Dawn—not to the body on the bed, but to *Dawn*, okay? Does that make any sense?"

I shook my head no. Tom sighed.

"I keep forgetting, you're new to all of this, that's why you didn't give us more trouble earlier. Okay, it's not your fault, you just don't know. And with that other demon here we didn't get a chance to tell you what's happening. Well, let me put it as simply as possible for you: Dawn's possessed."

"Fuck you," I snarled.

"Sam, I know how you feel, but this isn't the time. She's still in danger. We've only got one chance to save her, and we need you there. I promise we'll explain everything as soon as we get a chance. But we have to get that demon out of her first, alright?"

I've always been kind of a superstitious guy. I didn't doubt that God and angels and demons and who knows what else existed, but it was a big jump from "they might" to "they do, and they're in your bedroom fuckin' up each other's shit as we speak."

I still hadn't been given a minute to figure out what was happening around me, but since it didn't look like I was going to get that minute any time soon I was gonna have to trust somebody. At least these guys were promising to do the only thing that I cared about doing at the moment: saving Dawn.

"Alright," I agreed, "Just tell me what to do." Tom helped me across the hall. Splintered wood and shattered glass crackled under our feet.

In the room, Andy was sitting on the bed holding Dawn's hand. He was talking to her in a slow, soothing voice. Dawn's eyes was still wide open, staring at the ceiling without seeing it. The window shades had been ripped from the wall and sunlight was streaming into the room onto the bed. Someone had put the white sheets back over Dawn even though there was blood stains on them now. All of the evil things I had seen around her before were gone, thrown off the bed away from her. The room smelled like there had been a fire or something, but there was no sign of it that I could see.

Tom helped me sit down on the edge of the bed. I caught sight of Doc Mayline in the corner where he'd landed. It hadn't really meant anything to me when Tom had told me that they had "cut off all its senses," but it came back to me when I saw what they had done to the body. Ears, eyes, nose, and—going by the blood trickling down his chin and onto his shirt— tongue, had all been hastily and rather messily removed.

But I was finally with Dawn and nothing, not even the mutilated corpse behind me, could distract me from my girl. When I picked up her hand and tucked it into my own rough palm, I saw that her skin was pink and hot against the damp sheets. She was sweating more than before, and there was literally steam rising off her body.

"Sam," Andy said quietly, "now's the time, man. Tell her everything. Say you love her. Let her know all the things you ever wanted to say but never did. It might be your last chance."

He let go of her hand and got off the bed. "We'll be right back."

I lay down on the bed beside Dawn and pulled her towards me, laying her head on my chest the way we always used to sleep together before we was sick. I wrapped my arms around her and I felt her body shudder, a long tremor running down to her toes. I tried to brush her hair back but it was so wet that it clung to my skin and caught in my fingers. "Dawn," I whispered, looking in her eyes. "Dawn, I need you."

Andy and Tom came back in with armfuls of pictures from around the house: her parents. My cat. Dawn and me on vacation. He put them all around us on the bed. I kept talking to her, telling her that I loved her, telling her that she was the only girl I'd ever been in love with. "And I know this ain't the right time for this kinda thing, but I want you to know that I wanna marry you."

I saw Tom and Andy exchange a look over us. I ignored it. I knew I sounded fuckin' stupid, but I didn't care anymore. I needed Dawn to hear me, needed her to know that I was done finding excuses.

"Don't be mad," I said to Dawn, "I'm not proposing now, I know you'd be pissed if I did something that stupid. I just want you to know that I'm ready. I wasn't before, I was putting it off, I was coasting along, but I'm not gonna do that any longer. I don't ever wanna lose you, Dawn."

She began to convulse in my arms. She screamed. It was a single cry that went on forever, filled with pain and terror and rage.

"Hold her!" Tom yelled, "Don't you dare let her go, Carpenter!" He and Andy were scrambling around the room, trying to keep all the things they had put around us from falling off of the bed.

"What's happening?" I yelled over Dawn's scream—and I could tell it was actually Dawn now, not whatever else I'd heard using her voice before.

"You're doing fine, man, just fine. Stay with her!" Andy yelled back.

"Dawn," I said, "Dawn, it's okay, I'm here. We're gonna be okay, baby, we're gonna be okay." I clung to her and told her that over and over, ignoring my own head that was telling me to *Shut up and stop lying to her. You know the truth; you know that after today, nothing is ever gonna be okay again.* But I shoved that black thing down and held on to my girl and sweated it out as she screamed in my ear and beat the mattress with her fists, kicking at the air like a little girl throwing a goddamn apocalypse of a tantrum.

And then all of that stopped and the scream cut off and she was crying, weeping, with her arms around me and her breasts and her legs pressed hard against me. "Sam," she tried to say, but her voice was so hoarse I could barely hear her, "Ohmygod, Sam, I love you too. I love you too, Sam, I love you too…"

Her voice trailed off, and I saw that she had fallen asleep.

Her face was peaceful now, but I was still too afraid of what might happen next to let go of her. I kept my arms locked around her as tightly as I could for a full minute, but when nothing happened, I finally gave in and loosened my grip. I felt weak and sick. My muscles felt like jelly and it was all I could do to lay there breathing. I cradled Dawn in my arms and wished for the world to just leave us alone.

I felt Andy's hand on my shoulder. "Sam, get up. We have to talk, man. There's some shit you need to hear."

"I wanna stay with her," I said.

"She's okay, buddy, you did it. She's saved. The bastard is gone. But now we have to clue you in on what's happening. And Dawn's going to sleep for a good long time, so her body can recover. I've seen it before. Come on, man." Andy tugged at me. I shrugged his hand off but I got up and followed him into the kitchen anyway.

We sat in the chairs and I looked at the two of them. For as happy as I guess we shoulda been, they both looked kinda upset about something.

"So," I began, "what the fuck?"

They laid it all out for me, and I listened. Neat as you like, if you could believe any of it: all kinds of shit they was telling me. Complicated too, layers and layers of mistaken knowledge that us humans only thought we knew.

"God, as you know him, does not exist," was one of the most basic facts.

Well okay, if that was true then my working theory up to this point—that Tom and Andy was angels of some sort, sent to fight back the goddamn demon hordes—went down the shitter. Through all of this, I kept as quiet as I could, asking questions only when they totally lost me, 'cause I knew that if I tried to say all I wanted to, they'd never get to the end.

And it was obvious from the way they was acting that they expected something from me.

Partway through, Tom got up and went across the hall into the bedroom again. "Where's he going?" I interrupted; I didn't trust any of these characters to be alone with Dawn.

Andy waved a hand at me. "Relax, man, he's just going to get the host's body from the bedroom."

I sat back, but I was still tense. Something in me just didn't like Tom all that much.

"Anyway," Andy went on, "like I was saying: no God. But that doesn't mean there's nothing up there, just not the smiling old man you grew up praying to." The rest was a bit much for me to follow clearly: there *is* a supernatural being, he said. Why shouldn't there be one? But why, in a universe consisting almost entirely of forces at odds with our existence, had humans decided to believe that any "god" being would be benevolent? And listening to him, I couldn't think of a reason against it that made a piss drop a sense. The one supernatural force he said they knew existed, if you really havta give it a name, is Satan.

The fucked up face of Doc Mayline—twisted, bloody, and cut to shit—appeared through the bead-curtain to my left.

I jumped nearly outta my skin at the sight of him there, but Andy was still sittin' at the table, pleasant as you please.

"God damn fat-ass motherfucker," Tom said from the

hallway, and it was then I saw that his arms was around the corpse. Tom lost his grip and the Doc pitched forward; I'd call it a face-plant, 'cept he didn't have a face anymore. When the body hit the floor, it made a wet sound like the time Andy and I dropped some kid's jack-o-lantern off a parking garage in grade school.

I picked my chair up off the floor. I could see that Tom and Andy was both enjoying my reaction, and that made me a little pissed. "Hey man, we're trying to have a conversation here," Andy said, still chuckling.

Tom wiped his forehead with his sleeve. "Why talk here?" he said, "Grab his arms and help me get him outside. You can talk and carry, can't you?"

Andy made a show of getting up and grabbing the Doc's arms. They heaved and got him an inch off the ground, but he *was* a fat motherfuker so in the end they slid him out on the floor instead and rolled him down the back steps.

The whole time they was arguing, 'cause I guess Tom disagreed with Andy about using the name "Satan" at all. He said it conjured up all the wrong Sunday school ideas. Then they remembered that I was there and talked at me about how the words "good" and "evil" don't really apply, how words like "food chain" and "prey" are a better fit. They got into philosophy a little: dualities, and how "good" and "evil" could only exist as opposite meanings of the other, so if there's no "good God" then there just *can't* be a "evil Satan," can there? "Antonyms," Andy said at one point, but I think he was just trying to sound smart. It was all beyond me, anyhow, and I think they was both talking more to reassure themselves that they knew all about it than to get it across to me.

It was sunny outside still, with just a coupla clouds floating overhead and a slight breeze rustling some leaves. Real fucking beautiful, you know? I wasn't worried about anyone seeing us; I don't got a fence, but all the neighbors do so it's like the same thing. Spiky wood slats on one side, tall dark planks on the other, and chain-link behind. That way's the Roberts though, and they're never home.

"What are you gonna do with him?" I asked, looking around at the patchy yellow grass that was my yard. Actually, I shouldn't call what's behind Dawn and my's house a yard. We got a tree, a shed, and a patio—well, a cracked slab with chairs on it anyway. We don't go back there much.

Tom gave me this look like I was some kind a idiot. "He may have been possessed, but he was still a man. We're going to bury him, Carpenter, like a man deserves. Got any shovels?"

"Yeah, in the shed."

"Get them. We don't have that much time; we're going to have to get going soon."

I went into the shed to get the shovels. It was damp inside, and when I dug out the shovels I had to scrape the moss off their handles. The shed's one of those crappy pre-fab jobs on sleds. The wood's warping and the roof is worn out so everything gets moldy and rusty after it rains. We didn't even buy it; the Roberts had it for years but they was gonna throw it out when they got the fence put in, so Dawn and me pushed it onto our property instead.

Through the gaps in the wall, I could see them two outside. They was arguing about the best spot to bury the Doc. Andy was standing by the back of the house, but Tom was pointing to under the tree in the corner.

I leaned back against the far wall and took a second for myself, just trying to absorb it all.

So far, I got this much: there's a whole spiritual or whatever level of reality that we're only dimly aware of and that our science hasn't been able to investigate yet. And there are things, "demons" or "devils" or whatever you wanna call them, that live on that level against us sentient creatures. Feeding on us maybe, or just doing what we're doing, trying to survive. But the trick is that humankind grew up with them, so we have evolved some defenses. That's where our God comes in. "God" is just the name mankind has given to what is essentially an immune system we don't understand. It's a species-spanning belief, a defender that exists because all of us, even the atheists—who was right, by the way—believe in it.

But it's when that faith starts to fade that this parasite gets its chance. "The movies have it all wrong," Andy had told me when we was inside. "You know how possessed people get all sick, vomiting, fever, freaking out? That's not the demon controlling them, that's their body trying to fight off the infection."

I stepped out of the shed only to find them dragging the body over to me. I asked them what was going on.

"Tom saw that your shed is up on sleds. We figure we can push it a couple feet, dig a hole, and cover it up again. Sound good to you?"

"Uh, yeah, whatever." I hadn't really listened to him, I was still stuck on something else. They started digging. Andy looked up at me after a minute and musta realized how this all looked to me 'cause he got this real compassionate softness to his voice and told me to ask them anything I wanted to so it'd make sense to me. "Alright, then let me see if I've got this straight," I said. "Dawn lost faith, and one of the...demons...was trying to get in her and use her as a host?"

"Pretty much," Tom said over a shovelful of dirt. "And make no mistake, it *was* in her. But she never gave up hope. She never gave in to despair." He stuck the shovel in the dirt and put his hands on top of the handle, leaning towards me, staring into my eyes. "And we think that's the key, Sam, that's humanity's one hope at surviving: "evil" has to be invited in. It can stalk us and batter the gates and do everything you saw it do to Dawn, it can scare you, but it can't break through on its own. Our immune system is too well developed."

"Like Job, man," Andy said, stopping for a second to rub the stubble on his neck, "in the Bible." Tom nodded his head in agreement. I nodded to, 'cause I didn't want to look stupid even though I didn't really remember the story.

Tom went on. "You have to be the one to let it into your heart. But once you do," he glanced at Andy and then held my gaze with that same burning stare I'd seen earlier. "You're terminal." They went back to digging.

It was a good sermon. I could tell, 'cause I was fucking scared as piss at everything they had told me even if I only kinda understood what they was getting at with regards to me.

"How long did you say Dawn was sick like this?" Andy asked me after they'd gotten about two or three feet down. The two of them was working fast, making a real big hole for just this one dude, fat as he was.

I said, "Almost two weeks." He whistled, and I saw Tom's eyebrows go up.

"She's lucky, man. She's strong."

I smiled. "Yeah, I know. Hey, I got another question though."

"Shoot."

"What was Doc Mayline's part in all of this?" I asked. "I mean, I get that he was a host, but what I don't get is if the demon takes over, what happens to the person? What led him here?"

Tom said, "The person is still there, usually only barely aware that anything has happened, at first. It's not like a puppet. They control you the way a drug addiction does. You ever been addicted to anything, Carpenter?"

"Yeah," I said. I didn't tell them that I never kicked it. I knew exactly what they was talking about: the human mind is fuckin' crafty. It doesn't need step-by-step instructions, justa driving motivation. For the last coupla years mine had been a special blend of chemicals they call D'lilah. If you'd asked me to describe all the ways to get that shit, I couldn'ta done it. Thinking about it now, I don't know how I did. But every single time, no matter how tight money was or how much we owed, I've never not been able to find enough money or to call the right people to get a coupla tubes. That's how they were telling me these things worked into you, by giving you that need. It doesn't have to make sense and it doesn't have to be spelled out; as long as that need is there, burning in your head, you'll find a way to get it.

"That's how it starts, anyway," Tom went on. "And it can go on that way for months or years—depends on the host—

and little by little you're making the world a worse place for us and a better place for them. But then you get used to hearing those suggestions, you start forgetting that they're not your own. The demon figures out how to get to you, figures out what's most important to you, what you'd do anything for, and uses that. Then it's not long before you're in some poor bastard's house to help another demon convince Dawn's soul—or, you know, whatever—to give up, stop resisting, and let it in. That's what happened to your Doctor Mayline; somehow, his mind found a way to make all of that sound perfectly reasonable to him."

"You couldn't save him?" I asked. Now that they'd let me ask questions, I couldn't stop myself. I had to figure out what they wanted from me.

"We told you, once the host lets them in, there's no getting them out. We did all we could for him."

I pointed at the face of the corpse slumped against the shed. "Is that why you cut up his shit like that?"

"No," Tom said. "We did that because even though the host is dead, the demon could still be inside for a while, watching and listening. Learning about us; the ones that are fighting back. They have too many advantages on us already. We cut them up so they don't find out too much. So that maybe we'll still have a chance."

"Do they talk to each other? Are they following orders or what?"

"We don't think so. If that were the case, they'd be much better organized. Hunts like ours keep surprising them though, so they must operate the same way we do: team up as they find each other on earth, work alone if they have to."

"Well, if you guys aren't angels, what are you? Exorcists? Demon hunters? What?" I asked.

They stopped digging and leaned on their shovels again. "Fair question," Tom said. "Andy, you want to answer this one?"

Andy smiled. "This is where it gets a bit more complicated, Sam, so stay with us on this: Tom and I are already possessed."

If I was a smarter man, or if I'd had a goddamn minute to think about it, I would've figured that out already. As it was, I was caught with my dick out. I looked at Andy. "Last year," I guessed. "You tried to kill yourself."

He nodded. "Yeah, and not long after is when I got taken."

I looked at Tom.

"Six months ago," he said. He smiled like he was embarrassed. "Lost my job. Took it pretty hard."

I felt panic bubbling up inside me but I shoved it back down. "But you're not under their control," I said carefully.

"Not yet," Andy corrected me. "You can get good at suppressing their influence, hold them off for a while. But you can't get rid of them, not without taking yourself out of the equation. Sooner or later, we're lost souls. That's why demon hunting is a transitive position, Sam. To hunt them, you *have* to be one of them, and that means you've got an expiration date."

I said, "I don't follow, why do you have to be possessed?"

"Oh, there are plenty of reasons: It's easier to track them, easier to identify them. But mostly it's because you can't hunt them if you don't believe in them, and if you *do* believe in them, then you also know the truth: you know that God doesn't exist."

It was finally starting to come together for me. "And if you know that," I said, "then you've lost your protection. If they find you, they take you."

They was both staring at me now, waiting for me to get it. Then I really began to put it together. The hair on my neck stood on end. I said, "If that's so, then how come you're telling me all this?"

Andy sighed. "Sam, that's just the thing..."

"You been sick recently, Carpenter?" Tom interrupted. I became suddenly aware of that undersized elephant gun he was packing.

I answered him slowly. "Coupla weeks ago."

"And how long were you sick?"

"Seven days," I said. It had been two, but I was embarrassed about that since they had been impressed by Dawn's two weeks. And fuck them anyway, I hadn't had any way of knowing what was going on.

Honestly, I was surprised at how calmly I was able to accept what they was telling me. Maybe it's because it explained the last coupla weeks so well. Maybe it was because I was just too goddamn tired to be anything but numb any more.

"Not bad," said Tom.

"I'm sorry, man," Andy said quietly, "I wish we could have helped you. We only got on the trail of these three about a week ago. I didn't know one of them was you until you answered the door."

Three, he'd said. Franks. "Did you get Franks already?" I asked. They looked confused. "The guy at the lumber yard," I explained.

"Oh. Yeah, we got him last night."

"Shit," I said. I walked away from 'em then, back towards the house.

"Carpenter, where you going?" I heard Tom call from behind me.

"Gettin' a drink," I told them. Andy said something to Tom, but I didn't hear what.

I got inside and out of sight of them before collapsing into a chair at the kitchen table. My hands was shaking where they gripped the chrome edge of the table and I needed to take a hit off *something*, but I didn't have anything in the house.

I took some long, slow breaths. It helped.

Almost an hour had passed since Tom put the first bullet through Doc Mayline. No cops yet, which meant by now that nobody was coming. Maybe no one had heard, but more likely my neighbors just didn't want the cops sniffing around. It wasn't the first time there'd been gunshots 'round here without local law getting involved.

Pushing up, I went over to the bedroom and looked in on my baby. She was still sleeping like they'd said she would, recovering. But there was life in her face now and the barest smile on her lips. She was lying right in a sunbeam and she looked goddamn gorgeous; innocent and clean even with the guts on the walls and the splintered wood sticking outta the door frame.

I felt bad that she'd never know what happened to me, but I didn't see any way around it, not if I wanted to keep her safe. I was possessed; I couldn't stay with her.

Back in the kitchen, I filled some plastic cups with water to take to Tom and Andy. Looking down, I saw the long smears of the Doc's blood stretching from the hallway to the back door. I had to laugh a little; the blood was still wet, and the color matched Dawn's 50's accents fucking perfectly.

I went back out into the sunlight, squinting.

Ignoring the gut feelings I was beginning to recognize as the opinion of my own demon, I felt okay with my death. At least I wouldn't hurt anyone else. They were right, I'd already almost damned my girlfriend without even knowing I was doing it. Like they said, they'd needed me to save her because even though I was already taken, Dawn still loved me. It was being reminded of that love that brought her back, that kept her from giving in to the despair the Doc had been surrounding her with, and to give her the strength to reject the parasite clawing its way into her. But now that she was safe, I wasn't needed any more. And I was strangely okay with that.

I handed them their cups and took a look down from the edge of the pit. The hole was deep enough and plenty big. They was almost done. The Doc's body was six feet down, bloody eye sockets staring at the sun. In the heat, he was already startin' to stink. All that was left was for them to shoot me, dump me in on top of him, and cover us up. Dawn'd never know what happened, but she'd be safe.

I took one last look at the house where my girl was sleeping, then back to what was gonna be my grave. *Shitty place to be buried*, I thought. *Rotting on top of a fat guy. Fuck it, so long as*

Dawn's safe, I can deal with it. I looked at Tom and Andy. "Alright," I said, "I'm ready."

They looked at each other confused.

"For what, man?" Andy asked.

All my fake confidence went down the shitter. "Isn't it, uh, my turn or whatever?" Them two laughed in my face. I backed away from the hole.

"No, dumbass," Andy said, "it's mine."

"What?"

"We gave ourselves six months. You should have about five left yourself, if it took them a week to crack you. Sometimes it takes longer than that, sometimes a whole lot less, but it's safer not to push it. My times up. You're my replacement, if you want it. Thomas here'll be your guiding hand of justice, until he reaches his time. That's how we learn this stuff, that's how we fight back. I look at it this way: once it's over, that's it, man. So why not do as much good as you can, while you can?"

"Yeah," Tom agreed, a thin smile smeared across his face. He put one hand on my shoulder, trying to be brotherly or something. It wasn't working. "If the demon's only had you for a month, you've got some time before someone will have to put you down. That is, unless you're a real pussy or something. You see, this way you can take a few of the bastards with you on your way out, send them back to wherever the hell they came from."

So that was their offer. I'd been wrong earlier; they was proslatizing after all. It was kinda funny, really.

They kept talking, but I was starting to see that Andy was talking just to cover up how upset he was. I'd been so concerned with my own shit that I didn't even register what he'd just said: it was his turn to die.

That's why they'd dug the hole so big; room for two. Maybe three, if I didn't go along with their plan.

The more they talked, the less interested I became. They was missing the whole goddamn point. If there was no God, if the whole universe was out to get us and this is all there is, then what the hell do I care about saving anyone else? Save them from what? We're all fucked, either way.

Andy and Tom didn't want to risk another gunshot, 'specially not outside. In the end they decided that Tom would just choke out Andy, and we'd off him then. Crush his windpipe or something, I don't know. Whatever we did it was gonna be brutal, and we didn't have a ton of quiet options.

Tom grabbed Andy before he could have second thoughts. It went fine, I guess. I didn't feel anything as I watched Andy die. He'd tried to off himself a year ago, so what difference did it make that it happened now?

But something did click in my head as I stood in the shadow of the shed and watched Tom dump Andy's body on top of the Doc's. I knew that Dawn wasn't safe yet. I knew I needed to protect her. I couldn't do that if I wasn't with her, could I?

It's like I was thinking before: we're all fucked, either way.

So what does that mean, then?

That means it's all about me and the ones I love, which is Dawn. That means if I leave her behind so I can go with Tom, I still fucking lose.

I picked up the shovel beside me.

Andy taking the road he did made sense. He'd always had a chip on his shoulder, always been up for a fight when it was smarter to lay off. That was never me, though, and either way I'm not gonna leave Dawn again till I have to.

I hit Tom across the back of the head, hard. I felt his skull give way to the old steel. He never saw it coming.

I don't need any more proof than today that the love between her and me's real. It saved her, didn't it? And I proved that it's still *me* in here, not this goddamn demon. Not yet. With what Andy and Tom told me, I can watch for the signs—odd behavior, rationalizing, and the rest—so I'll know when I start to slip. If they say I got some months before it really takes over then alright, Dawn and I got that long together, don't we? If that's all we get, then I'm not gonna run away from it any more.

The dirt packed down pretty good over them three. It was tough getting the shed back in place all alone, but I managed. I went back inside. Tom had let on that Dawn wouldn't remember much, so I just had to clean up the house and figure out how to explain the busted door and the other shit without, you know, telling her the rest.

Till death do us part. That phrase always bugged me. Supposedly we all believe in a hereafter, right? So why take a vow to end love with death? Just never rubbed me right.

It's different when you know that death is the end, when you know that heaven isn't up there waiting for you. For me, "till death do us part" has a whole new meaning. It means more. It means forever. It means as long as humanly possible, I'll love and honor and protect my girl. It means exactly what I wanna promise Dawn.

It was too bright in the bedroom where Dawn was sleeping. First thing I did, I hung a shade over the window to block out the sunlight, filling the room with darkness once more.

You know, so she could sleep better.

JEN, NOW

Linda stirred her tea and tried to decide how best to surprise her son Erik with the news. The wrinkles around her eyes softened as she appraised her son sitting across from her at the kitchen table. It was Sunday morning, and he had picked her up from church for breakfast at her house just like he had done every Sunday since he had accepted a job in Newgan and moved back into town.

Erik's face was obscured by the newspaper he was studying, but Linda didn't need to see him to know that on the other side of the grey pages his expression was just the same as it had been a decade ago, when he used to fan his high school textbooks across this very same wooden table and pore over them. Yes, he'd be there studying and she'd be washing dishes behind him or talking on the phone with Beth, because Beth still lived next door back then. And in the study Rick, Linda's husband, would be in his chair, rocking himself with his foot and reading a novel of some sort or another. She always said he'd die in that chair one day; she'd been wrong in the end. But that was two years ago now.

"Erik," she began, "something interesting happened at work just this last Friday."

Erik sighed, wrangling with the newspaper until it gave in and folded up. His brown eyes met hers. "What's her name?" he asked, his tone mockingly patient.

"What?"

"Mom, you work in the community center. Not once have you brought up your job of your own volition since I've been back in Newgan—not once!" he continued over her noise of protest "except when it has had something to do with a girl you want me to meet. And date, and marry, and give you some grandchildren; preferably a granddaughter who I'll name Mary, after your mother.

"So out with it, Mom. I'm twenty-seven and I'm not getting any younger. She my age this time? Or out of college at least?" He said it all with a good-natured grin. Linda shouldn't have kidded herself that she could surprise him, as this discussion wasn't exactly breaking new ground.

Dropping her pretense of indignation, Linda allowed herself to smile back. "Rick was eight years older than me when he and I got married, you know."

"Yes, Mom, I know that. But Dad was thirty-six, which is not the same as twenty-seven and nineteen."

"Alright, alright. But that one was very cute, you can't deny the truth of that."

"Hmph. I bet you can't even remember 'that one's' name, can you?"

Outside, the full green leaves rustled on the branches as an April wind rolled through the Midwestern town. In the fall, the citizens would be electing their first town manager because the town had grown so much in the last few years.

"Well." Linda said, "Fine. I may not remember that one, but I know this one."

Erik got up and went to the sink to pour the last of his coffee out. He rinsed out the blue mug. "Still listening," he said, to make it clear that he wasn't.

"Jennifer Sonners."

There was the reaction Linda had been waiting for, a response other than Erik's usual bemused banter. It was nothing more sinister than the nature of life, one generation surpassing another, but it had been some years since her son had looked at his mother searching for answers that he didn't already know.

The moment didn't last long, but it was enough to satisfy her. Erik picked up his jaw and went on toweling off his mug. "Jennifer? What is she doing in town again?"

Linda launched herself wholeheartedly into relaying every detail that her supervisor Cary had told her at the center. It should have been a short story really, especially since Erik already knew most of it, like that Jennifer had been born in the nearby city. The only part he didn't know was what Jennifer had done after college when she moved to Arizona to work, and what had made her come back to her long-abandoned hometown now.

Erik let Linda go on without interruption. He wasn't really in the kitchen anymore; he was four years back in time, at college again. That was where he'd first met Jennifer Sonners, where their relationship had begun and ended in the span of two years. But he'd never gotten over that girl, as his mom rightly suspected. What Linda didn't know was to what extent Erik had loved Jennifer, or the way that his love had fossilized in the intervening years until soft half-truths of love-blind perception had hardened into facts beyond the reality of who Jennifer had ever been to begin with.

"...and don't tell anyone," Linda finished, "but I snitched her cellular number from her résumé for you." She thrust a fluorescent yellow post-it in Erik's direction like it was made of gold.

"Good idea, Mom, that won't be awkward for me to explain at all." He put his mug in an overhead cupboard and accepted the phone number.

The moment Linda had reveled in before had passed by completely now, but she wasn't disappointed. He'd dried that mug for a good two minutes, long after it was bone-dry. If he was that distracted, she reasoned, then she had been right and he was still interested. This was her best chance yet to have a granddaughter named Mary.

Linda had witnessed the symptoms of her only son's feelings, even if she didn't understand what drove them. It went unspoken every time, but the girls since Jennifer had all been dumped for, at least as far as she knew, terrible reasons. Not that he really told her about it, she just pieced together what she could from the stories she dragged out of him over the phone or on Sundays like this when she had a captive audience. The girls she'd been introduced to had all seemed nice enough, but before even two months had passed, the relationship would be over. She was afraid that it was because of Jennifer's ghost; none of the others could measure up to his memory of her.

"Are you going to call her?" Linda asked, surprised at how timid her voice sounded even to herself. She wanted grandkids, sure, but she also wanted Erik to be happy.

He flipped the note between his fingers. "I don't know. Maybe in a day or two."

"Erik, can I tell you something? It's about Rick."

Erik sat back down at the table, forgetting his own concerns for a moment. It had been a few years since his dad had died and although Linda kept a smile on her face, he had promised himself that he would be there to talk if she needed him.

"Sure."

Linda let out a long breath and stared at the wedding band she still wore. "Now don't get mad at me for this, just let me talk and see if it means anything to you." She waited until he gave a sign that he was taking her seriously. "Rick said something to me once about love that I want you to think about."

Before she could continue, there was a knock at the front door at the other end of the house and Erik went to answer it. He passed by Rick's recliner, still unmoved since his death, and the bookshelf behind it with all the adventure tales his father had loved. From where he stood he could see a girl's profile obscured by cream-colored lace curtain. She was looking away from the house into the side yard, surveying the neighborhood of Erik's formative years.

Erik had always thought Jennifer looked most beautiful in profile. After the break up, whenever he thought of her there was only one image that came to mind, one picture that he held onto: Her back towards him but her head turning to face him, the first rays of a self-assured smirk only just dawning, pinning her cheek up in place. In his mind the long arc of her face was mirrored by the lines of her hair which hung, poised, on the point of her shoulder so that with the passing of just one more moment, one more breath, it would spill over across the smooth expanse of her back like golden silk over pale ivory.

In the intervening years he had never allowed that moment to pass. He had tried to preserve that image against the acidic world in which real people lived. Now, she was here, in front of him. When he opened that door, there wouldn't be anything to stop the moment from coming. She would turn her head and look at him and he would have to say something to her.

"Who is it?" he heard Linda call from where she still sat in the kitchen. "Should I make up some more coffee?"

"Yeah, go ahead." Erik's pulse was up and he felt like he was back in high school, more nervous than he'd ever been in college. "It's Jennifer."

Even though she was nothing more than a fuzzy outline through the window, he could see who she was now and who she had been were not the same. He pulled the door open in one motion and tried to smile.

From the kitchen Linda could hear the two walking towards her through the house, talking like old friends but with a kind of forced familiarity, like they had both been hoping someone else would be on the other side of the door.

As they walked in, Linda put a big smile on her face. "Hello, Jennifer. My, you look lovely today!"

"Thank you, Linda," Jennifer said.

Where he stood, Erik jolted a little; Jennifer used to call his mom "Mrs. Letner." But he supposed they did work together now, so it would be different.

"I'm sorry to drop in like this. I just needed to drop something off for you. I didn't think anyone would be home."

"Oh, that's fine, dear. We were just enjoying the morning anyway. Would you like some coffee?"

Jennifer waved a hand. "Oh, no. I won't impose on you. Here, this is what I came by for." She set a yellow shoebox on the table. Its sides bulged with whatever it was holding.

Linda took the top off and pulled a few photos out.

"Oh! You found the pictures from the Spring Parade! But this could've waited until tomorrow, you didn't have to drive all the way over here."

Jennifer blushed. "Well, I knew you were looking for them so when I came across them I just thought—"

Linda cut her off, exclaiming "Look at me! Questioning kindness. What's wrong with me? But please sit with me and don't go running off so quickly. Erik"—she smacked him on the arm—"Get this young woman a chair from the other room."

"Really, Linda," Jennifer said, moving towards the front door. "I can't stay, but thank you for the offer. It was nice seeing you again, Erik." She had made it sound like she was about to walk out, but it was clear from the way her body hesitated that there was something more she wanted to say.

"Let me walk you out then," Erik said, shaking off his lingering bewilderment at Jennifer's re-entry in his life and regaining his usual attitude of dominance. The two retraced their steps through the living room to the porch. Outside, they said goodbye like friends and she walked down the sidewalk to her green SUV.

"Jennifer!" Erik called her back before she could climb in. He ran up and put his hand on her arm, trying very hard to make it seem friendly and natural when the reality was that just touching her sent his heart into overdrive. "I'd like to catch up more." He let his hand drop to his side.

He didn't know it, but his touch had sent her heart beating too. "That would be great! What did you have in mind?"

"Would dinner be too much to ask?"

"No, I'd love to."

They settled the rest of the details: Wednesday night, seven o'clock at Rita's. Rita's was Newgan's staple nice restaurant that forgave you if you didn't own a black tie. Jennifer drove home after giving Erik a quick peck on the cheek that put him nine miles high. Jennifer smiled the whole way back to her parent's house, where she was living until she found an apartment in town.

Erik did his best to hide his own smile when he rejoined his mother in her kitchen. To cover it up, he entered the room with a question. "You were going to say something before Jennifer stopped by, something that Dad said? What was it?"

"Oh, it was…nothing. Don't worry about it, dear."

Love is a science of dynamics, Rick had said to her, setting down whatever paperback he was reading at the time. That was what Linda had wanted to say to Erik out of fear that the Jennifer he was in love with didn't exist anymore. *It's too risky to fall in love with a person: people change.* Rick's unprovoked outburst was unforgettable because it was so unlike him; he was the type to sit quietly and observe. *It's rates of change, that's all.* He had continued. *Fall in love with the way a person changes instead. Then you've got something special: not one man and one woman that love each other for an instant, but a consecutive series of men and women that love each other for ever.*

You mean like us? Linda had asked with a little bit of a laugh in her voice, just in case he wasn't being as serious as he sounded. Rick had picked up his book again and continued reading without answering but now with a smile on his face unlike any she had seen there before. Linda had smiled too and thought it was sweet and ignored that it had happened, just like he did, until months later when he died and his words came back to her. It had taken Linda a while to decipher what it was he was talking about, and she never would know what had prompted the outburst of philosophical poetics.

* * *

Erik held the door for a family leaving Rita's, who smiled and thanked him before hurrying through the drizzle to their minivan. Although the weather was grey, Jennifer was glowing when the teenage hostess sat them at a table by the window. She was wearing a teal dress that she had accented with a matching black-stone necklace and bracelet set. She had laid out her outfit Monday and changed her mind three times a day since then. Erik, though not as bad, had almost been late when he spent five minutes retying his tie before deciding to leave it home and leave his collar open instead.

The restaurant seemed unusually busy for a Wednesday, the rush of busboys and the clatter of silverware sounding frantic for no apparent reason. They ordered, and ate, and talked long after the dessert plates were taken and wine glasses were empty. She told him all about her time in Arizona, and why she had returned home. He told her about moving back and as much as he tried to stay away from the topic, she got out of him what had happened to his father and what his mother had gone through. It was, after all, a large part of why he was working in Newgan.

"So that's why you didn't go to Indy, like you used to want to." She had said it as if it were a revelation.

"Still want to," he had corrected her, forgetting himself for a moment. The conversation had moved on in search of happier topics.

They had fun. Most of the time they spent laughing, or warming themselves in memories of their school days. But both of them were aware that those days were past them. Those times, that love, were other people in another place.

Driving to his own house, Erik tried to come to terms with this new girl. In many ways she was the same: she'd gained the weight that only the early twenties are excused from, but other than that she was still pretty, still living on the happy side of happy-go-lucky. *No illusions*, he thought, *we both know the truth. She used to love the person she saw in me, that I could become. But now she sees that I'm not that person.*

The rain had let off, but the roads were still slick. Erik kept his speed down, braking early at the red lights. *And she isn't what I remember, either.* It was hard to even define what had changed, but the fact was that when love exists, it is undeniable. And when it does not, its absence is just as impossible to ignore.

Her name, Erik thought. *I always loved her name: Jennifer is so long and regal and proud.* The garage door closed behind his car, sealing out the damp night.

"Please," she had said when he told her how beautiful she looked as they climbed into his car. "It's 'Jen,' now."

MEDIUM

The artist explains his latest piece to the gathered critics.

As you can see, most of this piece is common enough—carbon, oxygen, hydrogen, etc. Even the canvas itself is similar to many of the other planets I have worked on before. I began this project as I had the others, shaping the environment and placing my creatures on it wherever it pleased me. But this time, even as I worked, I knew I would not be happy with the piece if I went on as planned.

The forms were unique and new, yes, and the ecological balance was complex and interesting enough, but the overall result was—well, boring. I had done it all before, and so had many others, the exact same way. It was becoming routine; art should never be routine.

It is not the form that is at fault here, it is we, the artists. We must put aside our old standards and strike out in new directions, as we have in the past. Remember when we first began the technical art of world building? How difficult it seemed, how time consuming? Now, it is merely the first step on a longer list. But emotion-weaving is a finer art, an expressive one, and it must not follow the same narrow path.

The techniques and the guidelines that we have been relying on as we painted these worlds with life must adapt and evolve. The efforts of the past were good for their time and served to teach us much. But be honest with yourselves; after witnessing *this*, can you deny that the others were of tragically limited design?

It was in reflecting on my last work, *Joy*, that I conceived of all that I show you here today. The crucial axiom to remember is simple: it is variety alone that gives meaning to consistency. A singer's ability to hit a high note is impressive, but one note is not a song.

Joy is guiltier than most of violating this rule. That world was hailed for how well it expressed such pure emotion through the life upon it. A few slips of the brush showed, some pain here and there, but that all was deemed unavoidable in a galaxy governed by inflexible rules. While there is nothing wrong with expressing pure emotion in itself, I came to understand that it is both a benchmark and a dead end. If followed further, it will only stagnate the art. There is no variety in a pure emotion, and because of this it lacks for meaning.

And this art is capable of so much more than that.

Once I had conceptualized this, my whole viewpoint changed. The pain of "Joy" was suddenly its most interesting asset because it provided the only variation in the entire piece. I began intentionally incorporating more pain into my new project, thinking to expand on it more fully, but quickly realized that it was not the solution I sought. It helped the feel of the work, but it seemed too amateur a fix for such a fundamental problem; there was no substance to it.

So then the problem became how to create the variety I sought. I pondered over what I could tinker with, the variables that were at play. I created species after species, hoping that one would give me a clue to the answer. At last, I found a variable so few had ever manipulated that its existence was largely forgotten. I realized that neither I nor any of the other artists I know of have ever made creatures that were aware that they were alive and, as a corollary, were not aware that they would die. Such a creation has been avoided, I think, because it is too risky; the artist who tried would be risking his control over the piece, which negates his ability to claim it as his own.

Something told me that my answer lay in that one little variable, so I took that risk. My goal was variance; is it not reasonable to presume that variance would occur from a loss of control? Well, I was curious enough to think so. I left my other creatures to die and began an entirely new set.

My first attempt was to go to the other extreme; I made creatures that had knowledge instead of ignorance. At the time, I thought I would get opposite results. As it turned out, I was right. Too right. The result was what I should have expected. Opposite, yes, but just as stale. These new species, these naiads and golems and the rest, given knowledge of their death, its time, place, and cause, were filled with pure sorrow instead of pure joy. Death-fixation afflicted each and every one; what pleasure could they have when all their time was spent counting the seconds that remained to them?

So yes, they were different, but no less static and no more interesting than their precursors had been. The emotions were reversed but the results were the same. Boring. Static. Invariable, even on an individual scale. It didn't matter what the emotion was, the problem was that it was set in advance— a single, inescapable result stemming from the setting.

But my efforts were not wasted. I forged on, still strong in my faith that the answer was related to this variable, somehow. It was only after a few more failed attempts that I realized that the efforts at the extremes had inadvertently defined a range, and a range has, of necessity, a median. So I began work within this third option. What I had learned was that the spices of knowledge and ignorance are too strong on their own, that they must be blended if they are to be enjoyed. Perhaps even beyond the sum of their parts.

I began to work again, molding a new species and imbuing it with knowledge and ignorance both: the knowledge of their own death, the ignorance of when, how, and why.

I found that the results were even better than I had expected. My creature knew not just joy and sorrow, but something else as well, something new. Unlike the first set, this being could think about the coming of these things, could dream about joy and could fear the sorrow. Unlike the second set, it was forced to wonder about these things when it looked to the future, because it did not know when or what would happen to it and those that it cared for.

That, my fellows, is the secret to the piece you absorb even now; that unique feel, that flavor, that texture, is the uncertain future. Potentiality. Dynamicity. And most importantly, the byproduct of the two, catalyzed through this little being: worry.

I think it is the most beautiful thing I have ever created. Something new that varies not just as a whole, but from creature to creature.

I have worked in the medium of life for a long, long time, but only now, with *Worry* complete at last, do I begin to feel satisfied.

No other world I have ever made is worth looking at more than once. *Worry* is different; I feel as though I could watch this world spin until the stars burn black, and it is time to begin again.

FORGIVE ME, FATHER

The Call had been more a feeling than an actual sound. It had glided down a mountain and rolled over hills, through creek and cleft to find him. It had looked in his fields, his barn, even his small shrine at the limit of his lands. The Call had at last found him sleeping in his bed. It had been nearly midnight. He'd had no way of knowing about the forces at work in his world then, or of the terrible events that would befall him in only a few days. He'd had no way of knowing that his quest would end in what many would view as mankind's ultimate tragedy, or that he alone would be held responsible for it.

The holy presence had not disturbed his wife nor any of his four children. The farmer, skin tanned by years of hard, honest work, had sat up in bed with eyes wide when he felt the summons. Not for a second had he doubted what he had felt. Not for a second had he hesitated with what he had to do. He had dressed quickly in the dark bedroom, putting on a simple tunic and loose, faded pants. He took his best robe as well, but this he carried rolled up so that it would be clean when he reached his destination. His wife had smiled in her sleep when he kissed her. Before leaving the house, he had lit a candle as he recited the prayer of protection for his family, asking the flame to watch them in his stead. He had done the same for his land when he had passed the small shrine he'd erected at the corner of his property.

Lighting the candle there had sparked the proud memory of the day he had built that shrine, ten years ago. He had been twenty-five years old at the time and his new wife was a month passed her twenty-second birthday. The wedding had been beautiful and grand, with guests from the other side of Valley: a full two days journey. Their union had been planned far in advance. At her birth, before his family's farm and name were destroyed by the fire, her parents and his had signed the contract.

The farmer had walked into the night as he thought about his past, encouraged onwards by the pull of the Call. He had felt no fear though he knew the dangers that lived in the forests lining the main road. That night the beasts had slept, and the full moon alone had watched in silence as the farmer made steady progress beneath the cloudy sky.

The fire. Even though his parents and both his siblings had survived, it had destroyed their family name. His father's shoulders never seemed quite as square afterward, and although his mother tried to be happy, by his twelfth year the boy had realized it was just an act. When they went on the monthly trip to the town market, he would hear the older men muttering of the cursed family as their wagon passed. Once, after the family returned to their burnt land and small hovel, he had asked his father about it. He'd never seen his father cry before. He never asked about it again.

The farmer had been following the Call for over an hour and his strong legs had carried him far past the boundaries of his property, into the foothills of the Mountain Sacred.

No one but his parents knew why the family had been punished, but everyone knew that their god must have a reason, that some terrible sin must have been committed. Even as his family had struggled to survive without workable land, his promised bride's family had flourished. The girl had been the most beautiful in all of Valley and the promised bride to the first born of a family publicly disgraced by their god. His eventual marriage was saved by two things. The first was that her family was old and honorable and would not dare commit the greatest sin their society knew: the breaking of a signed contract. The second reason was that as soon as he was old enough to comprehend the reason his family name was spoken only in whispers behind his back, he had striven to become the most devout man anyone had ever seen in Valley. Whatever his parent's sin had been, none doubted the boy's ability to atone for it.

He had listened to the sounds of his sandals slapping against his feet as he followed the summons faithfully. The air had felt warm, with the promise of intense heat come morning. The farmer had covered many miles as another hour had passed and still the Call did not relent but instead urged him forward. He hadn't felt tired or weary. He had kept his mind active with memories from his past, softening the hard path he walked now with images from the paths he had traveled before.

After the marriage celebration, his bride had taken him to his new land. It was enough to put honor back into his family name, if he put in the work. The unbroken fields were not close to town, but the soil was good and it was a generous gift. They had gone on to build their house and farm and family. Their first construction had been the small shrine along the wide old road that bordered the edge of his new family hold. He'd selected each stone with care, and he had asked her to paint the simulacrum within. She had worked meticulously, knowing how much it meant to him. Every single day the farmer had cleaned and stocked the shrine with candles for anyone who sought to pray. When their first born boy had turned seven, the farmer had passed the sacred chore on. Like his father, the boy never missed a day. Travelers and merchants who passed called it the Shrine of the Narrow Path. The name came not from the road they themselves traversed, but because of the road the farmer who had built the shrine followed. Many stopped to say a prayer and all bowed their heads as they passed; some in respect of the god and some in respect of the man.

The third hour had passed him somewhere along the road, and the farmer had reached the base of Mountain Sacred at last. The Call had summoned him into the woods when the road turned aside to begin its lengthy climb to the summit. He'd walked through the forests, and had gone on as the ground sloped upwards beneath his creaking sandals. He had followed as the dirt turned to rock and the forest had thinned and ultimately disappeared except for a few bushes that held desperately to the rocky soil.

It was from this timberline that he had first caught sight of the eternal fires that held the inky night away from the Great Temple. It was said that in all of Valley, no location brought man closer to his creator than at the summit of Mountain Sacred.

A short time later he was led into a river. The water was pure and cold but only as deep as his neck. He had crossed with his bundle held high above the water, and he had not allowed a single drop to touch it even as the currents had worked to confound his journey and sweep him down into the lake at the floor of Valley.

He had made the far bank as the first fingers of the sun had shone on the horizon and had begun their day's labor of pushing the sun to its zenith. A seemingly futile endeavor, since the evening would see the sun roll beneath the horizon again, yet one which brought light and life to the world.

The farmer had wanted to stop and rest on the wet, rocky bank but the Call had become more insistent, telling him he must go on. From where he'd stood, the only way to go on was to go up. So up he had gone, slinging his bundle across his back and removing his sandals before beginning the ascension. The face of the cliff was not quite vertical, but very nearly so. Had it been vertical he would probably not have made it to the top, although he would have tried. As it was the winds of the morning—fed by cold air at Valley bottom warming and rising under the sun—almost tore him from the mountain face. He was forced over and over again to sink his fingers as far as he could into the crags, imitating the plants he had left far behind him, waiting for the gusts to subside.

Unknown to the farmer, it was during one of these times that his wife had awakened. She had been dreaming of their childhood, growing up separately but knowing that one day they would be together. He was not a hard man to love, really. He was honest in everything he did and while that in itself infuriated her at times, their love truly was that simple. Sure they had fought, but they'd always forgiven each other afterward. After all, they were only human.

When she realized he was not in bed, she had searched the house. When it became clear he'd gone, she became afraid. Without knowing exactly why she did it, she woke their two sons and two daughters, dressed them, and led them to the shrine. She had once asked why he didn't build another shrine closer to the house. He had told her simply that when worship became too convenient, it ceased to be worship. The way he had said it was as a man thinking aloud, as if he always knew he had a reason but never knew what it was until she had prompted him to tell her. They'd only been married about half a year then and, though they had felt as if they loved each other before, this moment was a milestone in their marriage. They both realized the depth of their partnership, how they could give value to each other beyond themselves. The question was just as important as the answer, and each revelation was not his or hers but theirs.

When her children had completed their prayers at the shrine, they had gone back to the house to begin their daily chores. She was the last to leave the shrine.

Even as the last amen passed between the lips of his youngest daughter, the farmer was achieving the summit. He rolled onto his back, his bleeding fingers shaking from the exertion. It was well into morning now, and in the light of day he saw his own appearance. The Call had left him when his fingers had stretched over the lip of the abyss at last. He needed no more guidance now, for it was clear that the temple was his destination. His simple clothing was streaked in mud and shredded from the rocks. He cleaned his hands on the tattered shirt and opened the roll he had protected all night. Inside was his best clothing: a long robe dyed dark blue, the color of the night sky just before the eyes of the stars have opened. He changed into the robe and bound the waist with a silver chain his wife had bought for him on an anniversary. Like the robe, the chain was not particularly ornate but the material was pure and the design simple. To him that made it sacred.

The road ran between him and the front of the Great Temple, looping around and rejoining itself on the far side of the structure. Across the road he saw the eternal fires raging in the bowls of beaten iron. There were seven of them. Three stood along each of the side walls, like pillars of flame supporting the sky. The seventh stood directly in front of the middle of the door. Each bowl was held eight feet in the air by worked iron stands and immediately behind these vigilant guardians stood the Great Temple itself. The farmer had visited before, though not often. The path he had taken this time was unheard of. All pilgrims took the one road that led up the mountain, but it had been built before the temple. The builders had needed a road their wagons could climb to bring up cut stone and other materials from below. Because of this, the road twisted back and forth to cut the angle of ascent. Long detours had been shaped to avoid pinches and impassable terrain as well. Had he taken the road from his land, it would have taken him much closer to a day and a half to arrive.

The farmer stood in awe of man's accomplishment. The grey stone of the outer walls had been smoothed and polished so that they looked almost to be made of glass. Proud columns braced the overhanging edges of the steepled roof. Closing his eyes, he muttered a prayer of thankfulness for his safe arrival. He'd come up the east face of the mountain and the entrance of the temple looked north so he followed the road around the corner to the front. The iron-bound timbers of the door were opened outward and he had to pass very close to the seventh fire bowl to go inside. Even in the wind, he began to sweat from the intense radiant heat.

The eternal fires were a miracle in themselves. They'd been designed to hold fuel, and some said that originally a rotation of priests had intended to arrive every other day to refuel them. But the first service had been held before the fires had been lit, and when the opening ceremony ended, all seven fires had sprung up as one and had needed no fuel since that day, in the times of his father's father's father.

The interior of the temple was simply beautiful. Its design did not attempt to overpower the pilgrim by overloading them with frivolous detail when absolute majesty worked better. This was a house of worship. The interior walls were plain and polished like the outer walls, but the ceiling was a masterpiece of wood carving. In great panels, the planets and the moon hung in their spheres around the earth. He couldn't help thinking that the stars of the outer sphere were shining, even though he knew it was clever carving and polishing to reflect the light from outside.

The temple was one large room, with strong wooden pews taking most of the space. The farmer walked purposefully to the front of the temple and knelt before the great statue of his lord and creator. According to legend, a lone artist had cut the stone to bear the face of the god and when he had finished, after gazing at the beauty of his creation, he had walked out of the temple and leapt from the cliff, knowing he could never do anything as great as this for as long as he lived. The kneeling man knew this story and had told it to his children many times, though he doubted that there was any truth to it.

As he prayed at the feet of the statue, he became aware of his exhaustion. He was hungry, his hands and feet ached from the journey, and his knees hurt from resting on cold flagstone. But he had been summoned and would wait until he knew why before indulging in rest or relief.

Far below in Valley, life for the hundreds of families went on as usual. They worked and ate and learned and played. They gathered fish from the lake and wheat from the field. Even as the kneeling man forced thoughts of the physical from his mind and focused on loving his god with all his spirit, the people in Valley continued to laugh and cry and live and die, oblivious to the revelations that would soon change their world forever.

Shadows stretched longer as the sun began to fall behind the mountains. A field hand looked up just in time to see the great temple silhouetted in the glory of the dying light. Without knowing why, the laborer covered his eyes, as if ashamed to witness the spectacle of the setting sun.

Meanwhile, within the dim confines of the temple atop Mountain Sacred, the kneeling man was still praying, waiting for his purpose here to be shown to him. As it grew darker, he built fires in the smaller bowls that lay at the base of the statue. Wood was kept in supply by the priests, along with the tools necessary to make fire. It was forbidden to disturb the fires outside. He struck flint to get a spark, and soon had light and warmth. As he tended to a fire beneath the god's form, a shadow of movement caught his eye.

"You have come at last," said a voice from outside the reaches of the fire. Unlike the Call, this voice was actually a sound, deep and resonating. The man thought that he heard a note of excitement in the voice, though he could not be certain.

"You've served me best of all my creations," the god said, "and because I know that it has not been easy for you and yours, I want you to know that I am thankful."

The man had knelt beside the fire when he heard the voice, afraid to respond, afraid to look.

"Do you know your purpose here, man?"

"No, my Lord," the farmer said, struggling to find his voice, "I simply heard and obeyed."

"As I knew you would. But do not fear, human, you will know your purpose sooner than you will want. For now, rise and face me. I must talk with you, my son."

"Yes, Lord." He stood and hesitantly turned towards the darkness. A robed figure materialized out of the gloom, pushing the hood back to reveal joyous, bright eyes and aging pale skin. The hands that laid back the hood looked strong. In fact, the avatar appeared exactly as the artist had depicted him in stone.

The god and the man walked outside. It was dark now and clouds had obscured the sky. Next to him, the man heard a soft sigh and watched in wonder as the clouds parted to let the moon and stars spill their light into Valley.

They walked on into the cold air of the evening. The man was still coming to terms with standing beside his creator, but did not want to rush his god into explaining himself. They followed the road around the temple, completing a full circle in the tomb-like quiet. As if resigning himself to action at last, the god spoke.

"Have you ever wondered about the world? Why I would make this universe, this planet, and all these beasts and people?"

A look from the corner of his eye saw a troubled expression on the man's face. "Speak freely, child," the god said. "You are my Chosen."

Bewildered by the title, the man repeated the lessons of the holy books. "We are taught that we exist for you, lord. To worship and love you and obey your laws."

At this the god chuckled. "Yes…my laws…" He did not speak for a long time, lost in thought. They continued to walk. They were along the south wall when the god regained his focus. "And of course, love. Your daughter has a doll your wife made for her. Would you say that she loves that doll?"

"Like a sister, Lord. She takes it with her everywhere, in the fields when I tell her not to, in bed, everywhere." The man smiled as he talked about the young girl, and the god smiled with him, but his smile bore with it the taint of sadness. The man did not notice in the dim light.

"And does the doll love your daughter back?"

"Of course not, how could it? It's just a doll."

"Just a doll indeed, but you have outlined the misery I have lived with for a very long time." He saw the smile drop from the man's face.

"No...do you mean that our love is meaningless, that we are incapable of love worthy of a god?"

"Quite contrary, it is I who am the doll and you who are the daughter."

"I don't understand."

"It is I who am not capable of love worthy of humankind. My greatest success, and still I fail you all."

The god, seeing the look on the face of his confused and distraught companion, began to explain.

"Let me tell you the story of your world. You must understand that to be a god is misery. I am not perfection or infinite wisdom, as you have been taught. No, I am just smart enough to know that I am incomplete, and just powerful enough to think I'm capable of fixing it.

"In the beginning, with the knowledge that I was lacking something, some concept or ability, I tried to find what it was that I lacked. To know what I was not, I had to define what I was. This was to be my tragedy, for in defining myself I bound myself by the laws of my own nature. I'm getting ahead of the story though; I did not realize what was happening until later. At the time I thought that although I could not conceive the abilities I did not have, perhaps the things I created could. Thus did I begin creating, so that my creations could find my answer for me. Light and dark, sky and sea, sun and stars, bird and beast, math and physics. Each new creation bound me further, yet from none of my creations could I learn the things I knew I was missing. I began to fear that a creation can never exceed its creator; that every being I made bore with it the very flaws I wished to rise above. I despaired."

They circled the temple again, following the well-worn road. In the back of his mind, the man sensed that it was getting darker out. He was too caught up in what he was hearing to consciously notice the change though. The deity, who knew full well the significance of the gathering gloom, continued to talk.

"But my efforts had unforeseen consequences: evolution. I did not make humankind the way I made everything else. You evolved from my other creations on your own, struggling to the surface by your very desire to exist. Born of my efforts but not of my mind, humanity's spirit was thus born outside of my laws. It was not long before I realized that this being was my last hope of ever reaching my goal. Humanity, the apple of my eye, was the answer to my question, a being capable all the things I was not: both love and destruction."

"You consider the ability to destroy a virtue?"

"Not in itself, but it is an ability I do not possess. Keep in mind that my goal was completeness, and the fruits of humanity are the abilities I do not have. It took me a very long time to learn what I am telling you now, but each stolen bite lent me knowledge into the potential of humankind. Potentials that are beyond me, for I am only a creator. What I'm saying is that the virtue of your species is not in the times that they destroy, but in the times they can and do not. That is why each of my previous creations had failed to answer my dilemma: not only could I not conceive of destruction, I did not realize that the ability to destroy is the natural prerequisite to forgiveness. Humankind's greatest virtue is forgiveness, and forgiveness is the decision not to destroy when one has the right and the ability to do so."

They turned a corner of the temple wall. As all that he had ever known of the world collapsed around him, the man interrupted, pleading desperately in the face of the truth, "But lord, you cannot really mean that humankind is above you!"

"You don't believe me? Then look at your own family, who were cursed by me. Look at what you yourself have had to do, how hard you've worked to rebuild your family's name. And why? Because of me. You have not heard the prayers of your parents as I have. You have not listened to their honest pleas for forgiveness every night until they died. But I cannot forgive, because I can only create. My laws defined my nature, and it is my unchangeable nature to avenge the breaking of my laws. I ruined your family mercilessly for it. Did you know that even at her death your mother still did not hate me? No, both your parents never stopped loving me. I still can't understand, and sadly I know now that I never will. How could I? I am only a god; they were human." The god smiled at the shocked expression on the man's face. They came around the temple again, finishing their fifth lap.

"When I realized what these differences were between humans and god, I saw how great humanity's potential was, and I was hopeful again." He paused. "Until I saw that I could never learn what I wanted from your kind."

They walked on in silence. Physically they walked abreast but mentally the man was far behind. The god stopped his lecturing to allow the man a chance to catch up. It was hard to tell time there on the mountain in the dark, but sooner than the god expected, the man spoke again.

"I think I am beginning to understand, Lord, although I am beginning to think that I do not want to understand."

"If that is so, then you must be on the right path. Let me tell you more of what I learned about humanity's unique status in the universe so that your choice will be easier to make when I offer it. To know right and wrong, you must first hear the knowledge that I have gained."

"I'm listening."

"Very well then. Human spirit, having been grown outside of my mind, could conceive the things that I could not. Yet the human body could not understand. The body was bound to my laws like everything else around it in the world. Humans acted at times in ways that even to them did not make sense, because my laws forcibly superimposed themselves on humanity's dual nature; the only beings capable of destruction, trying to reconcile their existence within a universe in which destruction was unknown. Constantly these forces moved against each other and, sensing this, I knew that humanity would not be able to achieve its full potential until my laws were gone. Only then would you be free at last to unite conception with understanding.

"But it was a long time before I figured all of this out. At first I thought only that humanity was my answer. I watched and shepherded my adopted creation. I began testing and experimenting, trying to understand your actions, your spirit. Trying to find what was so beyond my nature yet so central to yours."

"What sort of experiments?"

"Plagues, famines, things of that nature."

"Then—" The man hesitated, afraid to hear the answer. "Then what of the man we were taught was your son, whom you sent among us to teach us how to live a godly life?"

"He was my ultimate experiment. Though not my son, he was a man bred and sheltered and learned and experienced in such a way so that he would become the exemplum of all humanity's best and purest essence." The holy being chuckled in bitter humor at the memory.

"Your books have it backwards, human. I did not send him to you to learn godliness; you sent him to me to teach me humanity.

"That experiment failed, though not entirely. From him I learned that I cannot understand that which is beyond my very nature. But it was also from him that I first learned of humanity's ability to conceive beyond their understanding. When I realized what it was that stopped you from uniting the two, I knew that there was only one thing left to do. This was a hard lesson for me, for it meant that I could not be the one to do it.

"As I have told you, it is against my nature to destroy. I know it is my time to leave, and to take with me the laws of the world that prevent humankind from doing what I could not, from uniting his divided nature." He stopped walking, but did not look at the man. Instead, he gazed at his beautiful heavens, hanging above him.

"I am, and yet I should not be. I must die, but my very laws forbid me from passing."

The man understood. It was the conclusion he had begun to realize was inevitable.

"So you need one who is not bound by those laws, one born outside of them, one who can destroy. That is my purpose. You need me to kill you."

The god closed his eyes and let out a long, slow breath.

"Yes."

They passed the south wall and stopped near the same place the man had climbed up almost a full day ago.

"I won't do it."

"You will. You must. It is the only way your race will be able to grow."

"But my whole life I have worshiped you!" It was a weak, meritless plea and he knew it even as he gave it voice. The god looked him square in the face.

"And I live in misery of knowing I'll never understand why you love me as you do, despite what I have done to you. But I have chosen you to do it. I can't make you, of course. It is your choice alone to make. I have given you all the knowledge that I have learned and you must act of your own free will, as humankind always has, whether or not you knew it. It is what allows your kind alone hope of escaping from my boundaries."

"But why me? Why not any other human in Valley?"

"Humanity must break its own chains. No other creation is capable. Why you specifically? Because despite my punishments and trials, you have succeeded in personifying the greatest ability of humanity. You have never held your family's woes against me. You have always loved me. I chose you because you are a good man, the living epitome of man's *un*holy value: all that is not me. And I chose you for my own selfish reason as well. I chose you because someone will have to explain to all the daughters of men why their dolls can't love them back."

The man took a few steps away.

109

The god let him go, knowing that this was not an easy choice to commit to. He watched the man, consumed by nervous energy, walk around the temple again.

The farmer had listened as all the teachings were turned upside down. He did not doubt his god. He did not want to do this thing, yet what he was told made too much sense and he could think of no other option. He tried to comprehend eternal agony of watching dreams without being able to be part of them. He tried to imagine what he would do if it was *his* existence that was suffocating his children. By the end of his seventh circle, the man had made up his mind.

"What must I do, Lord?"

With the man's words, the god's shoulders visibly relaxed. He had been worried that the man would refuse.

"It is almost done already, human. The fires that surround this temple have burnt with my spirit ever since the temple was first built. These fires were created by me so that when I found the right man he would be able to destroy them. Look around; most of them are dark now. Each question rings as horns in my ears, and with each question you ask of your god, you extinguish another fire. With each answer, I return that part of my spirit to this body. Look behind you at the walls of the temple: they are crumbling away, their very foundations shaken beyond repair, like all the lessons of your childhood. Soon the walls will collapse and the temple will cease to exist. There is only one more question to ask, one more decision to make, and one more action to take. Even as we speak, all that remains of me is what you think you see in the darkness: the shadow of a god."

The shadow walked towards the edge of the cliff the man had climbed. He spread his arms and held high his head. "Do you wonder how the artist who carved my image came so close to the truth? It was not divine inspiration, there is no such thing as that. Far greater, it was his own human inspiration that conceived such a heroic vision of a god. I made myself in the image man made for me.

"Even now I want nothing more than to emulate that artist of so long ago. My creation is all that I am not, and I will never create anything greater. I should leave—" His shoulders dropped. He turned to look at the man. "But I cannot do it. Only a human can banish me completely."

"What will happen when you are gone?"

"I do not know exactly what effects my death will have, but you will adapt and survive, as you always have. It will take time, but my laws will fade. Then, it will be humanity's time to grow." There was a fatherly smile on the god's face: pride mixed with sadness.

Hesitantly, the man approached. He wanted to grieve, but he knew that he must respect the sanctity of the existence he was about to end. He could not stop his tears, but he did not look away from the kind face atop the cliff. Feeling that it was right, he hugged the robed figure out of sudden fear of the new world that would come with the sunrise.

"This sacrifice…it's a very human thing to do, Lord." He whispered, unable to speak any louder through the tightness in his throat. He kissed the god on the cheek.

Then the man put his hand on the chest of his god and, very lightly, pushed.

With the slightest of exertions he destroyed his creator. All that had been needed was an act, a decision by the only being able to destroy. The god fell slowly, seeming almost to float down the cliff face. His body began deteriorating as the air rushed by. First, the robe unraveled into dust, followed soon after by the being inside who seemed to loosen and grey, the dust and ashes spreading out as what once was a holy deity became nothing more than an expanding dark cloud. The crying man turned and began the long walk home. Behind him, the cloud continued to grow.

* * *

The farmer's wife saw a man sitting in front of the shrine praying. It was her husband, who had been missing for three

111

days. He was wearing his best robe, but she could see that it was creased and muddy. With tears of relief in her eyes she ran to him and threw her arms around his neck, covering him with kisses.

"I've been so worried!" The words tumbled from her mouth. "Where have you been? Why didn't you tell me where you were going?"

"I…"

She realized he was not smiling back. His eyes were red and his skin was pale.

"Loved one, what did you do?"

He told everything, every little detail his tormented mind could recall. She listened, clinging tighter as he told the sad story.

"Then you did what you had to." She tried to console him but she was still in shock at his words. She did not doubt the truth of what he had told her. "There was no other option. It was what he wanted."

"No, it was what he thought he wanted. But he was wrong; I smiled when I killed him."

She stared at her husband. Her joy, at first transfigured into disbelief, grew into horror.

"I didn't want to, but something in me couldn't help it. Something in me was elated that at last my family had revenge. He said himself that he was the source of all our pain and struggle."

She had known many people, good men and women all, who had died because of the god's "experimental" plagues and famines. She wondered if she would have done the same as her husband, or if anyone at all would have been able to truly forgive actions that had robbed so many people of happiness. Her mind and body felt cold.

"I thought I had forgiven him, even he thought so, but it was never true!" Her husband screamed in fury at the very nature of what had happened. "It is still his law, still his nature that overshadows my desire. I'm just another flawed creation, we are all flawed creations. Humankind's only virtue is camouflage: we're just better at hiding our flaws than the others. Do you see? Do you understand? He called humanity his greatest success and he died thinking that. He never knew what we were. He died freeing a mistake!"

She could not speak. There was nothing to say. After a while she realized she was sitting in the dusty road, her whole body numb.

"I understand. But now that he is gone...what do we do?"

"That's what I've been trying to figure out my whole trip back. We have to leave." He pointed towards Mountain Sacred. "See that cloud? It isn't going away. We can't live here anymore."

Over the next few days, the farmer gathered his family and spread word that everyone had to leave Valley as quickly as possible. Some called him prophet at first, but it was not long before everyone but his family called him devil. He had not accepted their offerings and he did not defend himself from their accusations. He just repeated that it was time to leave. As the black cloud had spread without any sign of dissipating, the families had taken what they could and fled. By the sunset of the seventh day, Valley was devoid of life and light. The sun could not penetrate the shadow of the dark cloud that hung permanently over all of Valley.

In the Outer Lands, the world was beginning to change in inexplicable ways. The humans tried to rebuild the society they had known, but now they had to fight the land for food and their prayers went unanswered.

When the farmer died, none but his family attended the funeral. His sons built a pyre at the entrance to Valley and laid the tired shadow of their father across the dried pine. His daughter, fourteen now, had heard his story from her mother many times. She brought her old doll and set it by her father's hand. Her mother set the fire and they all stood back to watch. The fire caught quickly, spreading to coat the whole pathway in purging flame. After an hour of silent vigil, his sons returned to their own wives and families and farms. When his daughter left, the fire still showed no sign of dying. The last to leave was his wife.

The man she loved never came back from Mountain Sacred, she thought. In the years that had passed they had spoken rarely. He'd been unable to stand living around people and as soon as the new lands of his family had been established he had left them all to live alone. She had visited him every once in a while, after her anger at his desertion had faded. They never spoke. They would just sit until she left. Now, as she watched the blades of flame consume the body of her husband, she realized there was one thing that might have saved her husband, one thing she had never said to him.

Early on she had tried to console him. She had tried telling him that he could not blame himself, that it had all been part of their god's plan. Her husband had never listened because she had never said what he needed to hear most. After a while she had stopped trying to help him. That was when he left, and when she began to hate him.

She had been blinded by her emotions then. But now that he was gone, she felt she knew the words that might have brought him back to her. She knelt, her long hair falling forward to hide her face. Even if she had missed her chance, she still wanted to say the words out loud.

"Maybe you are right, and it is not in any man or woman to forgive the god who did this to us and to you, my love." She felt as if she could barely breathe. "But I am your wife, and you are my husband. I know these words are too late, but I hope, somehow, you can hear them: I forgive you—"

Her words, swathed in tears, fell to the dusty earth. The wind carried the dust to the fire, and the rising air delivered the last of her words to the heavens above: "—and I will always love you, Cain."

The farmer's wife stood and turned her back to the flames that would burn forever, blocking the entrance to the Valley of the Shadow of Death. She walked into the Outer Lands; into the new world of humankind.

HI, MY NAME IS GRACE
-a play in one act-

Characters:

Grace - Forlorn character. Has been waiting a long time to be in a story.

Character 2 - Newly created character. Speaks more formally and politely than Grace.

Setting:

The blank canvas within an author's mind.

*[Lights up on **Grace** sitting on empty stage. **Grace** sighs. Rising, she approaches the edge of the stage, keeping her eyes fixed down as if looking into an abyss. She seems nervous about what she is doing. Behind her in shadow, **Character 2** walks briskly across the stage. **Grace** glances back without much interest. After a moment, **Character 2** walks back on stage wearing a somewhat different outfit, pauses, goes offstage again. This time, **Grace** watches with more interest and her gaze lingers towards where **Character 2** disappeared.]*

Grace *[looking straight up]*:

You gotta get started sometime, man.

[Hopeful beat. **Grace** *shrugs and again focuses her gaze at the floor off the end of the stage.]*

*[***Character 2***, again with a slightly different outfit, wanders to the middle of the stage behind* **Grace** *and stops, looking around in wonder.]*

Grace:

He must like you.

Character 2:

What?

Grace:

I said, he must like you. You've been back and forth here a couple times now.

Character 2:

Have I?

Grace *[laughing]*:

Yeah, back and forth, in and out. I'd wager he doesn't even have a plot yet.

Character 2 *[uncertainly]*:

Oh, I see. *[Beat]* May I ask, who "he" is?

Grace *[gesturing at everything]*:

The author.

Character 2:

Ohhh, okay. Thank you for explaining. *[Beat]* And, who are you?

Grace *[considers the abyss off the edge of the stage again, then visibly makes a decision and approaches* **Character 2** *instead, away from the edge]*:

Hi, my name is Grace. Nice to meet you.

*[***Grace*** *shakes* ***Character 2's*** *hand]*

Character 2:

It's nice to meet you too, Grace. One last question, if I may?

Grace:

Shoot.

Character 2:

It's just that…well…who am I?

Grace *[looks at her mismatched outfit up and down]*:

From the looks of it, you're nobody yet. *[Character 2 looks distraught]* It's okay! I'm not really anybody either. He's never put me on paper, so everything could still change.

Character 2:

I don't much like not having a name.

Grace:

I know the feeling. Don't worry, he'll get around to it. If you like, sometimes you can push him a little. Try concentrating really hard on that question: "What's my name?" I think it helps sometimes.

Character 2:

Does it?

Grace:

Well I mean, it hasn't gotten me outta here yet, but I think it works. Here, watch me. *[Grace looks intensely focused. Character 2 walks around her, studying. Grace opens her eyes and smiles, pointing offstage]* There! It worked that time! *[Grace crosses to the side of the stage, retrieves a chair and takes a seat]* Now you try.

Character 2:

Very well then. *[Character 2 concentrates]*

Grace:

And I'll see if I can get us some more furniture.

[Both Grace and Character 2 look concentrated, eyes squeezed shut]

Character 2:

Olivia! Amanda! April! Susan!

Grace:

Table! *[opens one eye, peers offstage, retrieves a table]*

Character 2:

…Denise! Candy! Archibald!

Grace *[pausing]*:

Archibald? That's not a girl's name!

Character 2 *[in a horrified whisper]*:

My name is Archibald?

Grace:

Now don't you sweat it, Archie, he probably just thinks that's funny. He goes through a lot of bad ideas before he gets anything good, believe you me. Keep pushing him.

[Character 2 resumes shouting girl's names]

Grace: Chair! *[Opens eyes, looks around. Nothing this time]* Chair! Ah, there we go! *[Retrieves a second chair from offstage]*

Character 2:

…Katie Lee…Olivia…Olivia… *[Opening her eyes, excited]* My name is Olivia!

Grace *[smiling]*:

See! That's a beautiful name. Now come on over and take a load off, Olivia.

Olivia:

I feel so much better now that I have a name. I really can't thank you enough for your help, Grace.

Grace:

Don't worry about it. My pleasure.

*[They sit in silence. **Grace**, patient. **Olivia** tries, but after a few moments gets fidgety]*

Olivia:

Grace, what are we doing here?

Grace *[with certainty]*:

Christmas.

Olivia:

Christmas?

Grace:

Christmas.

[Beat]

Olivia:

Pardon my language, but what in the blue blazes does that mean?

Grace:

Beats me. But I'm afraid that that's all that he's got so far. You, me, and Christmas.

Olivia:

Well that doesn't sound like much of a story to me.

Grace:

Shhhhhh not so loud. He might agree with you and give up. Then we'll never get out of here.

Olivia *[eyeing **Grace**]*:

You seem to know quite a lot for a nobody with nothing but a name.

Grace *[distant and haunted]*:

Well, I've had a long time to figure it all out.

Olivia:

How long?

*[**Grace** doesn't answer]*

Olivia *[with intensity]*:

How long, Grace?

Grace *[still distant]*:

I'm not sure, exactly. Time passes strangely sometimes, but…I've seen a lot of others go out there. Maybe…18 stories? 20? I've been here all that time just…waiting…

Olivia:

I see. I'm sorry to hear that.

Grace *[with somewhat forced optimism]*:

Naw, it's fine, you're okay. It's hard sometimes, but I have faith. He's written some alright stuff. He's not great, but he's good. I'll get out there someday.

Olivia *[trying to brighten things up again]*:

Well at least you've got me now, right?

Grace *[not particularly convinced]*:

Sure.

Olivia:

What's the matter, Grace? Do I annoy you?

Grace:

No, no, nothing like that. It's just that I've seen a lot of others already go out into the world, most of them that he came up with after me. It just doesn't seem fair sometimes, you know?

[Everything seems to shake as if in a small earthquake]

*[**Grace** jumps up, gripping the table, trying to hold it back as it is pulled offstage by unseen forces. The table disappears and **Grace** lets go]*

Grace:

No! Give it back! Write about me, you doofus! No one wants to hear about a table!

Olivia *[scared]*:

What was that?

Grace *[angry, pacing the stage]*:

Another one! Another one complete, and I'm still here!

Olivia:

I don't understand, what happened?

Grace *[defeated]*:

He finished another story.

Olivia:

But, I didn't see anyone else come through here.

Grace:

Really? Because the hero just made a grand exit from our world and a grand entrance into theirs.

Olivia:

You're referring to…the table?

Grace:

Yeah, it was an "experimental" piece of fiction. No characters, nothing really happens, just an idea piece about a table. He writes things like that sometimes when he gets frustrated. He won't make a penny on it and no one will ever read it, but he calls it "art" and puts it out there just the same.

Olivia:

Well then why do you care?

Grace:

It's the principle of the thing!

Olivia:

Grace, sit down. If you're honest with yourself, you'd know you don't want to be in an experimental piece with a table. If I may, I'd say you're afraid.

Grace:

Me? Afraid? Ha! What would I be afraid of?

Olivia:

That you'll never get out there. That no one will ever get to meet you. That you'll die here, having never lived, having never made someone laugh, or cry, or witness their world in a way they never have before.

Grace *[stunned]*:

How did you know?

Olivia:

Because I've only been here an hour or two and that's how I feel already. I can't imagine what it's been like for you, waiting all this time.

Grace:

Olivia, I'm sorry I got angry like that. It's just…it's just…it's hard to keep my hopes up.

Olivia:

Grace, you said he's good but not great, didn't you?

Grace:

I said that, yeah.

Olivia:

And you're still here, right? After what, twenty stories since he thought of you?

Grace *[pointing to where the table exited]*:

Twenty-one now. Why, what are you getting at?

Olivia:

I just want you to realize that you're here, in his head. He likes you, Grace. He's just waiting for the right story. The longer the wait, the better he gets. Maybe you'll be his masterpiece one day.

Grace *[considers, smiles a little]*:

You're a quick study, Olivia. Thank you.

Olivia:

I had a good teacher. *[Winks at Grace]* Not great, but good.

[They both stand and begin taking off a layer or two of clothing, revealing different clothes underneath. They seem not to be in control of their own bodies]

Olivia:

What's this, now?

Grace:

He's fine-tuning us. Don't worry, it won't be anything major.

Olivia:

Grace, I'm still worried.

Grace *[still changing]*:

Don't be. Look, what's your favorite color?

Olivia:

Orange.

Grace *[as **Olivia** is still changing something]*:

Alright, and let me ask you this then: What's your favorite color?

Olivia:

My favorite color? Why, it's green.

Grace:

There, you see? Writers are always being told these details matter so they waste a lot of time messing with them, but you're not any less Olivia for liking green.

Olivia *[abashedly]*:

Actually I prefer blue now.

Grace:

Uh...well it is disorienting while it's going on, I'll give you that.

[They stop changing and achieve normal looking final outfits. They sit]

Grace:

See? All that fuss without moving the plot forward at all.

Olivia:

What plot?

Grace:

Exactly! *[Yelling upward at author]* What plot?

Olivia*[shooting to her feet]*:

It's a story about hope!

Grace *[also coming to her feet, excited]*:

Well I guess I'll have to eat my words, he is making progress! And?

Olivia:

And...and that's it for now. But he knows that much.

Grace:

A Christmas story about hope. That's mighty original. Sheesh.

Olivia:

Indeed. I'm starting to understand why you've been here so long.

Grace:

Right? No plot, not much of a setting, and—If I'm lucky—two characters.

Olivia:

Well, if he can write about a table then I trust he'll be able to think of something for us.

Grace:

He's just lucky we don't age in here, that's all I've got to say. Here, let's try this. [**Grace** *stands, places chair with its back on the ground, and sits in it, staring up*]

Olivia:

What good does that do?

Grace:

It's an exercise. We take what we've got so far and move it around, try to see things from a different angle. Maybe it'll help him get some ideas and get us out of here.

Olivia:

I suppose it can't hurt. [*Olivia places her chair on its side and "sits" in it*]

[*They wait*]

Olivia:

Grace, I was wrong. It can hurt; my neck is starting to ache.

Grace:

That's nothing, my butt's gone numb.

[*They rearrange themselves in different, still incorrect ways*]

Grace:

I get the feeling that it's not working.

[*They right their chairs and then take seats again*]

Olivia *[as they are righting their chairs]*:

Something else did occur to me while I was sideways though.

Grace:

What's that?

Olivia:

I think you're right about him; he's not that great yet. Maybe he never will be. But I do think he's clever. I can't help but believe that he'll find a way to tell your story, Grace. You've just got to trust that he loves us and that he might have to put us through a lot, but that in the end, he cares about us.

Grace:

Oh, I've got no doubts about that. He's an artist, which means that he loves himself. And he made us, so we're part him. We're loved by extension.

[They chuckle together]

Grace *[more seriously and quietly]*:

You're right though. I get frustrated, but I've never really lost hope. Hope is something he gave me, and it's kept me going so far.

Olivia:

That's a pleasant sentiment. I agree with it—but I don't believe that you do. *[**Grace** looks at her surprised]*

I think you're lying to me, Grace. I need to ask you something and I hope you'll forgive my forwardness.

Grace *[eyeing **Olivia** somewhat suspiciously now]*:

Shoot.

Olivia *[looks away from **Grace** and takes a deep breath]*:

What were you doing when I came in?

*[**Grace** looks away, doesn't answer]*

Olivia:

You were standing at the edge over there, staring into the darkness. *[With more intensity]* What were you thinking about when I came in, Grace?

Grace *[resigned]*:

I was…I was thinking about getting myself out of here.

Olivia:

That's what I was afraid of. *[Olivia glances nervously at the edge]* Would that work?

Grace:

I don't know. I was thinking maybe it was worth a try.

*[**Grace** approaches the edge again and stares down. **Olivia**, somewhat afraid of the edge, joins her]*

Olivia:

Let me ask you this, if I may—

Grace *[smirking]*:

You know what? You ask a lot of questions.

*[**Olivia** smiles]*

Olivia:

That's because you give such interesting answers. But tell me, have you ever talked it all out like this before?

*[**Grace** thinks]*

Grace:

No, not really.

Olivia:

So just as you were having this crisis, I appeared?

Grace *[still staring into the abyss]*:

Uh…yeah, pretty much.

Olivia:

Interesting. *[**Olivia** looks up, sees the audience]* I think your time is closer than you realize.

Grace:

Hmm?

Olivia:

Look up, Grace.

*[**Grace** looks up, sees the audience watching her. A look of speechless joy comes over her face.]*

Olivia *[reverently]*:

He did it, Grace. It's been your story all along. It's like Christmas, in a way; one sent to save another. A story of despair. A story of hope. A story of answered prayers.

Grace:

Olivia-

Olivia:

Yes, Grace?

*[**Grace** starts to offer her hand, then thinks better of it and hugs **Olivia** instead]*

Grace:

Thank you.

*[**Olivia** straightens **Grace**'s clothes and brushes her hair into place]*

Olivia:

Go on, now. It's time.

*[**Grace** enters the audience, shaking hands and introducing herself to a number of people with "Hi, my name is Grace. It's so nice to finally meet you." as she makes her way to the back of the theater and out into the world she has waited so long to enter]*

[Lights down]

[End]

A NOTE FROM THE AUTHOR

I hope you enjoyed reading some of my stories. Please take just a moment to rate and review this book on Amazon. Due to the way Amazon is set up, every review contributes to making my work more accessible and easier for other readers to find.

The best way to buy more copies is through:
www.createspace.com/4973680

For information about upcoming releases visit:
www.stefanbarkow.com

ABOUT THE AUTHOR

Stefan Barkow lives in northern Indiana. He holds degrees from Purdue University in English literature and economics.

www.stefanbarkow.com

35387677R00080

Made in the USA
Charleston, SC
07 November 2014